A WORLD OF MISFITS

"This crossing to the space port, will it be dangerous?"

"Undoubtedly."

"Won't all the rest of your kind be glad to help?"

"Lady," I said, "ripping a kid out of his home, classifying him as something less than human, and shipping him trillions of miles through space to a backwater planet full of things that would just love to eat him does not make for a well-rounded personality. There are more total savages here than there are civilized people and about half of them can't remember any kind of life but this."

We will send you a free catalog on request. Any titles not in your local bookstore can be purchased by mail. Send the price of the book plus 50 cents shipping charge to Leisure Books, P.O. Box 511, Murray Hill Station, New York, N.Y. 10156-0511.

Titles currently in print are available for industrial and sales promotion at reduced rates. Address inquiries to Nordon Publications, Inc., Two Park Avenue, New York, N.Y. 10016, Attention: Premium Sales Department.

PLANET
OF
THE
GAWFS

Steve Vance

LEISURE BOOKS ✆ NEW YORK CITY

A LEISURE BOOK

Published by

Nordon Publications, Inc.
Two Park Avenue
New York, N.Y. 10016

Planet of the Gawfs

Prologue

1997 was a good year on Earth. Naturally, there was strife—a rebellion in Australia, the continued resistance to the abundant foodstuff Planktite by such groups as the Lord's Messengers and the divergent Hindus—but these problems were now looked upon as challenges, not impasses. The mere fact that human civilization had survived the collapse of the 1980's seemed to mature the race from swaggering blunderers to emerging explorers, from undisciplined eight-year-olds with dangerous toys to the wondering adolescents who tempered their ability with vision and reason.

The Solar Conversion Design publicized by the Costello Foundation in 1985 had won out over such yet powerful opposition as the United Petroleum complex and the Nuclear Visionaries and virtually eliminated the fouling of the atmosphere within two years. The development of low cost and plentiful nourishment from the oceans was instrumental in at least postponing the gigantic problem of what to feed nine billion human beings, even though the Voluntary Tempraster (temporary sterilization) and planned birth programs were still having a difficult time making any significant headway.

Then, in 1993, Alfred Skorzinik seemed to have cleared this last great hurdle and dragged mankind along with him. Earth, by then three quarters united in the International Federation, had established outposts on Luna, Mars, four asteroids, three of Jupiter's moons, and one of the satellites of Saturn, but faced the dismal prospect of confinement to one system due to the vast interstellar distances beyond the last planet. Even with the plus-ninety-per-cent light speed of the experimental Ramjets, the trip was just too long—until Skorzinik's faster than light Tachyon Drive was developed.

Suddenly the universe was open, and the world rejoiced. Staring up at the cold, distant, glittering night sky, this defeat of an unbreakable law had allowed the human body to race alongside the human imagination. A first round-trip to Centauri took eighteen months; a second trip ended in tragedy; but a third mission was successful in one year. The latter expedition established a base on a near Mars-like planet.

Strangely enough, supralight time corresponds within a few micro-seconds with sublight, thus eliminating the perplexing, often eerie effects of close-to-light speed travel, during which years can race by though perceived only as minutes aboard the vessel.

Most fortunate of all, however, was the discovery on the first 1996 expedition to the star Capella of a planet almost physically identical with Earth. Was this the prayed-for answer to overpopulation? Had a truly acceptable emigration world finally been found?

The planet was officially, and unimaginatively, labelled Earth B, but it soon came to be called Thear (a simple anagram of "Earth") by practically everyone. A full-scale expedition consisting of sixty of the world's finest scientific minds was preparing to answer the questions on everyone's tongue in late 1997 when Nature, in her own cruel fashion, stepped in to settle the problem of overpopulation.

As nearly as can be reconstructed, eleven-year-old Adrianna "Annie" Sanderson, the daughter of Lloyd B. Sanderson of Manchester, England, was playing with four friends in the backyard of her home on September 15, 1997 when she happened upon a mass of pale white material under a large tree. It seems to have been about the size of an orange and had the texture and consistency of liquid chocolate, sticking paste-like when touched.

Later that evening (most reports state about four to six hours later), Annie complained of vicious stomach cramps and fever, regurgitating repeatedly. Alarmed (her temperature seems to have climbed as high as .106), Mr. Sanderson, a widower, rushed his daughter to the local hospital for treatment. Annie probably began undergoing convulsions in the vehicle. By the time she reached the hospital, she was in a deep coma. Attending physician Robert Morgan was baffled by the girl's condition when his preliminary tests produced no expected results and his emergency measures failed to bring this condition under control.

Twenty minutes after Annie's admission to the hospital, Lloyd

Sanderson complained of a headache and breathing difficulty. Taken to a lounge area, he immediately began to vomit and experience violent convulsions. Annie died about then, not having lived more than fifty minutes after her initial symptoms. Lloyd died an hour later while undergoing treatment in the emergency ward.

While the general first opinion leaned toward poisoning of some sort, Dr. Morgan was sufficiently alarmed to insist on isolation of all those who had come in contact with the Sandersons. Unfortunately, staff shift had come just fifteen minutes before the elder Sanderson's death, and six known contactees had already left the hospital. When Dr. Morgan died ninety minutes later, the true depth of this misfortune was revealed. By morning, thirty bodies had accumulated, victims of what has since been called the Disease, God's Wrath, and, simply, the Plague.

Did it come from outer space with the Tachyon explorers? Was it brought back by the trips to Alpha Centauri or Capella? Was it a monstrous mutation of some known disease? These questions have not been fully answered to this day, though many investigators cite the unusual amount of meteorites landing in England that year, while others cling to the belief that recent digging in the Sanderson yard to set up proper drainage tiles uncovered some particularly virulent form of meningitis.

It seemed to survive on any form of recently animated organic matter and could be transmitted by a touch. The horrible death spread from Manchester in a stage of temporary dormancy, not striking down its host for as long as seventy-two hours on occasion. After only two days, the greatest plague since the Middle Ages had swept over and was ready to ravage a major portion of England.

How the disease crossed the Channel is another point beyond hope of clarification, though the obvious means of human transport offer themselves most readily. Within a month, the swift death had reached over the western half of the European continent and spread onward with undiminished fury. By October, the peoples of India and western Asia were engulfed in the devastation, often losing as many as three out of every four inhabitants in densely populated areas. The most advanced medical technology in the world still had delivered no other answer than complete isolation. No one of any age, sex, or race was immune. Consequently, the rising flood of terrified emigrants from the ravaged lands was met by hostile resistance, which sometimes went so far as mass murder on the borders of the receiving countries.

On October 9, 1997, the first case was reported in North

America, apparently smuggled across the Bering Strait by fleeing victims in illegally landed ships. While its progress was swift, its proportionate death toll was much less there, as the entire United States had been somewhat successful in reverting to armed isolation. However, looting, murder, and other related acts of violence soared.

On November 21, a young man in Mexico died from the disease. Exactly a month later, Brazil reported its first case.

Australia, generally thought to be providentially located, was hit hard and unexpectedly in late December, despite the inhabitants' fanatical policy of insulation and vigilance, and the planet's last large stronghold crumbled. Only the islands were left.

Horace MacClean was stricken in mid-January (either the 15th or 17th), 1998, in Los Angeles. His contact apparently came from a large dog that he killed and partially devoured. When the convulsions began, MacClean was immediately deserted by anyone who had been close to him at the time and left to die, writhing in the streets. What made this case so different was that the man convulsed, lapsed into a coma, and revived in just over an hour.

Informed officials approached the seemingly healthy old man cautiously and wore protective clothing. Tests proved that MacClean had, indeed, been a victim of the disease and had, more amazingly, survived. Swift action followed. The first recorded triumph over the Plague was thoroughly investigated by the hastily reformed, but powerful World Health Organization. A tentatively formulated vaccine was developed by using MacClean's own blood as its base and administered to Patricia Gellman in the early stages of her seizure two days later. The second success over the disease was recorded.

Mass production of the easily synthesized vaccine began, with the W. H. O. now Earth's only effective governing body. Distribution was a problem at first, as each of the six nations originally involved in the organization understandably wanted their own areas immunized first, but, by July of 1998, a substantial portion of the Earth's remaining population had been inoculated.

The vaccine could not stand off the attack of the still-raging Plague, but it did lessen the severity of the assault, and, in about eighty per cent of the known cases, it effectively prevented the death of the victim. Once afflicted, a survivor could not catch the disease again, though a few did become notorious as carriers.

October 27, 1998, stands out as a high point in the records of human survival. At ten-fifteen Pacific time, Robby Lewis of Oregon emerged from his coma and became the world's last authenticated Plague victim.

By this time, the W. H. O. was the most powerful governing body in the world, and in early 1999, Earth, its population drastically depleted, rested. That rest continued into late September.

Out of the nine billion human beings alive prior to the Plague, only three quarters of a billion remained. Of these survivors, at least six million (by W. H. O. statistics) had undergone a non-fatal bout with the disease. Scars had been left, not only the mental scars, but the invisible, insidious physical scars.

Of the children born to the affected parents in the months of September and October, one out of three was a monster.

A world reeling from the most massive depopulation in its history was struck while blind with pain, as thousands of helpless babies were brought into cold life mutated, deformed, and grotesque. Every conceivable caricature of the standard human form seemed represented by these genetically cursed children, and their parents, torn by love and horror, were often driven to the extremes of paranoic defensiveness or infanticide.

The World Health Organization literally controlled the remnants of civilization and felt it to be their duty to investigate this turn of events. A brief inquiry revealed that the families containing one affected parent stood the chance of having one mutated child in three, while families with two affected parents faced the awful prospect of one out of two being a mutant.

This told the anxious young couples what they had to fear while giving the world sons and daughters. As to this question, the W. H. O. replied, "Insufficient data at this time."

So the births continued, and the monsters came.

In 2000 A.D., James William Kurtz was an undistinguished biologist from somewhere in New Hampshire. He was one of the hundreds of young doctors who were members of the large W. H. O. experimental team assigned to the problems of the mutants. He had evidenced little or no socio-political aspirations when recruited by W. H. O. He impressed his reviewers as the private, curious loner who would welcome the chance to lose his identity in his work; for a time, he played his part well.

It wasn't until sometime in December of that year (records are spotty on this point), that Kurtz first uttered his now familiar anti-mutant declaration, "God's Blueprint only!" before a receptive audience. The gathering was the New York City chapter of the rapidly growing Parents for a Human Society, and Kurtz, as a representative of W. H. O., was the featured speaker. This was a period of hysterical rejection of the ever-increasing subpopulation of Gawfs (a slang term for mutants, "God-awful freaks"); this was especially true since such a high proportion of the little creatures were surviving. Unfortunate parents generally hid their offspring or retreated into the now numerous uninhabited areas. The Parents for a Human Society was a para-military group concerned with the Gawf problem who seriously considered extermination. (Incidentally, its members had never suffered the Plague)

Kurtz' statement about God's Blueprint referred to the bodily design of the average human being. Its enthusiastic reception immediately elevated Kurtz' public status and made him one of the most sought-after speakers in the world. Kurtz was actually a "softliner" in comparison with some of the more violently inclined representatives of the Parents; he advocated isolation of the young mutants, not wholesale slaughter.

Of course, most intelligent people came to regard the biologist and the Parents as reactionary dinosaurs whose own hate and ignorance would quickly devour them. But the group, with its policy of superiority and separation, contained some of the most eloquent and zealous individuals left to the human race. Quickly, viciously, the group expanded, becoming worldwide and acquiring such a number of influential converts that it was suddenly second only to W. H. O. in political power. Kurtz rose at an equal pace through the ranks of the World Health Organization; he stood at the doorway of the top office at the time of the first world elections.

Despite a desperate counterattack by opponents of his fanatical policies, James William Kurtz was voted as the director of W. H. O. on April 18, 2001. By August of that year, an Earth Congress that was eighty-five per cent Parents for a Human Society had increased his power to nearly that of a modern dictator. By October, the first colony for mutant children had been set up in Australia.

This was still too close for many militants, and a bomb blast in the colony on November 29 killed sixteen children and two directors. In January of 2002, the first supralight speed space vehicle departed for Thear, that mythical wilderness world circling the star Capella. It contained six hundred and eight mutated children (two years old and younger) and one hundred volunteers who were willing to live the remainder of their lives in exile with the unmourned outcasts of the human race.

The long and sad story of "The Planet of the Gawfs" had begun.

1

"Capture, Conviction, and Sentence"

"Nineteen years," I cursed silently as I huddled in the tiny crawlspace above my apartment, "nineteen years of beating the tests, lying, disguising myself. Oh God, not now!"

Below me, in the now dishevelled living room I had so proudly displayed to my parents and friends, three of the Black Troopers, henchmen of the W. H. O., casually tore down everything I'd worked for, while they questioned my father through their plastic smiles.

"Really now, Mr. Harper," I could hear one of the men say in his friendly, deadly voice, "we will find the boy whether you cooperate or not. Is that really a legitimate reason to risk six months of your accumulated vacation time?"

"You still don't believe me, do you?" I could also hear Dad reply. "I know of no freaks in this area who haven't already been captured by you fellows. How can I help you?"

I sweated in the blackness, praying that they would accept his word and leave, but knowing that they wouldn't.

"You are Daniel C. Harper, forty-three, of 3701 Carswell, correct?" the first man asked sternly.

"That's right."

"You have a nineteen-year-old son named Elias Blaine Harper?"

"That's also correct."

"And this nineteen-year-old male is a mutant who has unaccountably eluded detection by the Organizational devices?"

"Now that's not right. Eli is as normal as you are, officer. Whatever gave you the idea that he was a freak?"

"Report," the Trooper said. "An informant named Delvecci,

Stewart, stated that one Harper, Elias Blaine, was born affected, and since the deviation is a disguisable one, has never been so classified."

I clenched my fists. Stu Delvecci, whom I had trusted, grown up with...

"Hold on," my Dad was saying.

The Trooper verbally marched over him. "A routine check run by the reporting board revealed that E. B. Harper's last chromosome test was given over ten years ago, and the results were in fact forged. As a matter of policy, the board issued a call for Harper and when he failed to respond voluntarily, placed him on the fugitive list. Where is your son, Mr. Harper?"

"To begin with, Stu Delvecci is about as intelligent as a rock, and secondly, Eli is out of town for the week on a University junket..."

"The University has recorded no such trip. In fact, he is officially listed as truant."

I glanced nervously around, searching for the non-existent exit. If forced, I might be able to go through the wall into the next apartment, but that would be slow and noisy.

"So, Mr. Harper, in your own best interests, I suggest you tell us the location of your son."

Dad's voice was a snarl. "The hell I will."

Other ears might have missed the sound altogether, but my ears heard it for what it was: a fist striking a jaw. Dad gave a low grunt of pain as another muffled blow struck.

Self-control is not one of my strong points. Before I could stop myself, I had ripped the hidden ceiling door from its panel and was plunging down at the men below. One trooper drew his stunner and pointed it at me, while the others smiled confidently. Their plan had worked by driving me out of hiding, and now they were three trained W. H. O. troopers against two ordinary citizens, or so they thought.

The gun was ready to spit at me just as I reached out and tore it from the man's grasp, breaking two of his fingers. A punch to his face demolished his jaw and sent him spinning into the wall. Dad elbowed the trooper holding him in the gut and pulled free, as the last man tried to draw his stunner on me. I kicked the weapon away before he could clear the holster and backhanded him across the sofa.

The first trooper, his lower face a bleeding mess, and the man who had been holding Dad latched themselves on me like leeches, using various forms of Oriental fighting techniques. I peeled the first one off before the second hit me high in the back and sent the both of us to the floor in a welter of arms and legs. He was fast, strong, and well-trained; I was faster, stronger, and possessed a natural combative instinct in keeping with my deviation. It wasn't really a contest as I fast-pitched him into the nearest wall and stood to face the trooper who had done all of the talking.

"Elias Blaine Harper!" he practically screamed. "As an agent of the World Health Organization, I hereby place you under arrest for..."

I laughed as I lifted his squirming body and prepared to toss it through a large window that sat some six stories above the street.

"Stop it!" he was screaming now. "I command by the authority of the World Health Organization! Stop it, please!"

A loud, inarticulate grunt from behind made me turn my head while still holding the man aloft. It was the first trooper, and he couldn't talk because of the mush I'd made of his jaw, but I got the message clearly enough. He was holding Dad back with one arm about him and forcing a jagged piece of lamp against Dad's throat with his other hand.

"Hold it right there," he seemed to be grunting, "or this one gets a rip job."

"Dad," I said slowly.

"Run, damn it!" he shouted back. "Get out of here before they get their guns!"

But I couldn't, knowing that to run would personally drive the nails into his coffin. So, silently, I stood there, lowering the trooper until he hung from my right hand a couple of feet above the floor, and dropping him the remaining distance to land with a dull thud.

"Run," Dad was pleading, "my God, run!"

The third trooper found a usual stunner, and I watched numbly as he aimed it at me, pushed the plunger, and knocked me into sudden, chaotic oblivion.

Why I had ever thought that I, out of the hundreds of thousands of Plague mutants, could successfully dupe the W. H. O. storm troops and live out my life is as irrational and blind as human hope itself. My parents had produced two normal boys and a girl before I was born in June of 2008. At first I had seemed quite normal, also, since that was before required birth gene tests. Kurtz and his group had foolishly believed that loyal doctors and nurses would automatically turn in any obvious freaks. So it wasn't until my third year that the first signs of deviance appeared. As both of my parents

17

held well-paying jobs, they were able to disguise my symptoms, including bribing a doctor to falsify test records for school and paying a dentist to perform some tricky work on my teeth.

I grew rather typically, always subtly aware that I was not completely the same as my friends, but camouflaged well enough to get by. There were some things that I could not do in public under threat of dire punishment from my parents, but no major slip-ups had occurred previously.

I had finished school and begun my first year of university training of Knowledge Reclamation when, seeing my best friend pinned under his own car one afternoon, I had revealed my true nature and saved his life. The most improbable impossibility in my mind at that time had been that Stu Delvecci would report me to W. H. O., but he did, and they had finally trapped me after Dad and I had sneaked back into my old school apartment to pick up some forged travel and identity papers I was going to need in my new life as William Hedges.

And now my life *has* changed immeasurably.

I awoke slowly from the artificial sleep, with my thoughts and memories a jumbled alphabet soup in my brain. I wasn't in my own bed in my own room, but where . . . ?

"Well, the sleeping dog wakes," said a half-laughing voice next to my head.

I opened my eyes, looked around, and instantly realized that I was in a jail cell.

"You are, I take it, another poor, misbegotten soul finally tracked down by our ever-vigilant Gestapo and placed herewith in their constant, loving care." The speaker, my cellmate, was a tall and slender man of about my age, with blond hair and a bored look around his eyes.

With the supreme effort, I sat up on the cot and tried to hold my stomach together with my hands. "Yeah," I grunted, "whatever you said. Where am I, or is that too corny to answer?"

"No, quite reasonable, actually. You are in what is commonly referred to as the Tombs, a large underground city installation that was named after a prison. Not surprisingly, it was used as a jail in pre-Plague times, and, less surprisingly, it still is in post-Plague times. I'm Jeffrey Nichols, your partner in mutantcy." He extended his open hand.

I stared at the offered palm that wavered before my throbbing head and said, "Consider it shaken; I feel like I couldn't do anything with conviction right now."

"I know that feeling," Jeffrey Nichols replied. "Even though I swore that, as a physical coward, I wouldn't offer the slightest resistance, some trigger-happy joker stunned me for insurance. The effects will wear off quickly enough if you just sit still. Your next question has got to be what has happened to your clothes, am I right?"

I glanced at myself and found that, as he, I wore only a pair of green cloth shorts. "Okay, I'll buy that; what *did* happen to them?" No shoes, no shirt, just the shorts.

"They were obviously liberated from you while you snoozed and, most likely, burned."

"Burned?"

He nodded. "Many folks at good old W. H. O. take a very unscientific attitude concerning contact with us deviant types, usually washing themselves thoroughly and disposing of articles handled too long by our unclean hands and bodies."

Conceding to the wishes of a head that was, unfortunately, still attached to my body, I lay back down and closed my eyes. "So, now what happens?" I asked.

"We wait for our trials," was the answer. "A couple of doctors will come by someday soon and check us on the gene tests and, if the court's not too badly backed up, in a week or two we'll go before W. H. O. Judge Howard 'Shoot 'Em Off' Mackle. After that, it's Thear."

"What if I'm innocent, I mean, physically normal?"

"Apparently, you *could* pass," Jeff admitted, "but I hardly think a minor detail like normalcy would sway Shoot 'Em Off's decision. In four years, the man hasn't let a single soul off the hook."

"Great," I muttered.

"What is your, uh, difference, anyway?"

"Oh, you'll see in a couple of days. How about you?" I looked over at him.

And, smiling, he totally disappeared.

"Hey!" I shouted, coming to my feet.

He was suddenly back again, in the same spot with the same smile.

"You turned invisible!" I told him.

"Sort of," he admitted, "but not exactly. You've seen chameleons, I guess? Well, meet the biggest and most talented one in the world. I can blend into any color, pattern of colors, or texture

I've ever come across, sort of turning invisible in a way. I got happy-drunk last week and did it at a party. There were thirty-two reports on me by dawn."

"Real appreciative, weren't they? Does that protective coloration work at your command?"

"Oh, of course. And automatically, too, when I'm not careful to check it. By the by, I didn't catch your name during these ramblings."

"Harper," I said. "Call me Eli."

Jeff's estimation of our probable term of pre-trial confinement was fairly longer than the actual time. I learned later that pickings had been slim for the past week, and the deportation boys needed a few more bodies to fill out a shipment to Thear. For this reason, our examinations and trials took place the very next day following my arrival.

I had spent an uneasy night on one of the two cots, while the noises, stench, and closeness of the cell compounded my already tense disposition and allowed me only snatches of sleep. An armed guard patrolled the long hallway, looking carefully into each occupied cell with his too-bright flashlight and quieting the scared and crying or angry and shouting.

By morning, when we were ousted for a dismal breakfast slid in through the bars of the cage, I was in a bad humor. My fur had grown perceptively along my shoulders and arms, and long years of hiding my difference made this an uncomfortable situation. Jeff was more than a little surprised to see the thickening brown hair spreading toward the center of my back.

The doctor, accompanied by a guard, arrived at our cell before noon and quickly went through the preparations for the gene tests by selecting amounts of hair, skin, and blood from each of us. He then performed a few minor operations having to do with blood pressure and respiration.

"How did you manage to pass for nineteen years?" the doctor asked after doing a little test on my biceps.

"I'm a good actor," I replied in a mutter.

He saw my special dental work and, using a clamp-like tool, wrenched off the caps to expose my real teeth. They felt strange in my mouth, so smooth and sharp.

He left with our medical samples in appropriately marked plastic bags.

20

"So that's why you're in here," Jeff said in reference to my now obvious differences.

"That's part of it," I affirmed, and, wanting to change the subject, I added, "Wonder why none of my family has been here to see me, yet. I'm sure Dad knows where I was taken after they·tagged me."

Jeff shook his head. "Forget it. That's practically rule number one: 'Thou shalt not have visitors.'"

"You've seen your lawyer, of course," I said naively.

Jeff laughed out at that remark. "Lawyer? What do you think I'm in for, petty larceny?"

"What? But the Human Rights Bill of 1994 is still in effect, and it says that—"

"The Human Rights Bill applies to *humans*, Eli old buddy, and, like it or not, mutants are *not* considered human under the present system of W. H. O. laws."

"Come on! You mean, just because I have a little hair—"

"That's more than enough reason. I've heard stories of how Mackle has convicted extremely ugly suckers even though it was legally proven that neither of their parents had ever contracted the Plague."

"He's sentencing naturally deformed people to exile?"

"That's right. Helps breed out all of the bad traits in our race."

"That," I said, "puts me in a terrific mood. I'm sure I'll sleep like a baby rock tonight."

He shrugged.

But another surprise awaited us. The trials began that same evening.

I guess that about forty handcuffed, genetically affected deviants were in the courtroom that evening. They all looked to be fifteen or older, including one guy who was probably in his mid-twenties, about as old as any Plague-induced freak. On the whole, they appeared normal, but I figured that ninety per cent of all mutants captured in the last five years or so would have looked fairly average. Most of the grossly deformed children had been snatched up long ago.

Besides myself, some of the more spectacularly deviant "gawfs" were a boy with a third eye in his forehead (usually covered by bangs), a man with hair strands as thick as spaghetti (probably hidden by a wig on most occasions), a woman with ears the size of bananas (hair, again), and a slickly shiny green-skinned girl (don't ask me how she escaped detection).

A guard escorted me none too gently before the bench and instructed me to state my name, age, and address clearly to His Honor.

"Harper, Elias Blaine," I said boredly. "Aged nineteen years, eleven months, six days. Last address, 1408 Mather Drive, University of the World Library, West."

Mackle coughed and squinted at a sheet of paper he held before his face. "Yes, Mr. . . . uh, Mr. Harper, your record states that you have lived for the past nineteen years under fraudulent pretenses, specifically, passing as a genetically pure human being. You have even, at one point, falsified official World Health Organization records concerning your single previous gene test. Is this correct?"

"Yes," I answered quietly.

He read a few more lines, moving his lips silently. "You also . . . um, resisted arrest with some force."

"Yes."

"The sentence of this court, after careful deliberation, is that Elias Blain Harper shall be stripped of his citizenship of this nation and this planet and be deported along with others of his kind to Earth B in the star system Capella, there to remain until the termination of his natural life."

My jaw dropped a foot. Exile? After living this much of my life with no problems here on Earth? Jeff had called him Shoot 'Em Off Mackle, but I hadn't listened; I hadn't believed that anyone could be so coldly unfair.

Mackle waved absently at my guard. "Take him back to his cell and have him on the departing ship tomorrow."

Maybe it wouldn't be so bad. I mean, everyone has seen the films sent back from Thear, the rich, green land, the acres of farmed meadows, the agreeable climate and mild weather.

Try as I might, I couldn't convince myself that involuntary deportation to a planet other than the one I called home would turn out to be a blessing in disguise. It could have been the Valhalla of Norse legend and still have been abhorrent due to the fact that I was being exiled from my family, my friends, my whole way of life.

I sat on my cot and stared vacantly through the bars into the empty hallway. Of the forty people brought before Mackle that day, thirty-six of them would be boarding the ship for Thear the next afternoon with Jeff and myself. The two who escaped exile had been a young boy who had somehow gotten a private physician into the courtroom and a girl with a heart condition. The boy's doctor had sworn as a junior member of W. H. O. that the child had six fingers on each hand due to a "natural" inherited trait. He could remain on earth, said Mackle, if he had the offending sixth digits amputated.

The girl circumvented the Judge's sentence by collapsing before the bench and dying when she heard it.

"I don't particularly care to dress this way," Jeff was saying, "but I must admit that W. H. O. issue looks good on the female of the species. Did you see that girl who looked like she had plastic skin? I got severe precipitations of erotic fantasies just looking at her."

The girls and women were forced to wear outfits that looked like one piece bathing suits with short skirts. No shoes for them, either.

"Yeah, if I can find her once we get over there, maybe I'll just settle down in the bole of some big tree and go full steam into an immoral dissipation, from which I'll not emerge, but expire in a hundred years or so. Happily, I might add."

Though the universe seemed to be tumbling down around my ears, I had to laugh at this. "Nothing bothers you, does it?"

"Only the lack of women and leisure time, friend, both of which I intend to have an abundancy of after our transfer."

Still grinning, I lay back on my cot, and when the lights were switched out at nine, I closed my eyes and tried to sleep.

When you go on a trip of any length, it's only natural to pack up a large portion of your clothing and personal possessions, and, since this was to be the longest voyage of my life in terms of time and distance, I should have loaded trunks with the accumulation of nineteen years. That was one of the many minor anxieties chewing at me as I waited in the bright noonday sun to be shuttled along with almost seven hundred other mutants to the barge that was then orbiting Earth. My rapidly blistering back only served to magnify my misery.

I'd never seen so many freaks before in my life, though I was now officially one of them. Even in the warning films put out by W. H. O. urging affected adults to be sterilized and not conceive possibly deformed children, the mutants were only in isolated shots. This landing strip was a chained sea of distorted human forms: rainbows of colors; countless limbs and digits that were too numerous or too few on their hosts; a couple of guys who had to be ten feet tall; and six or seven perfectly formed "midgets" who were small enough to be carried in individual cages by normal men. But the center attraction among the mutants and thousands of curious onlookers from the nearby city was the young Oriental man who had two fully separated and functioning heads above his shoulders.

Ten shuttle craft capable of lifting seventy passengers each were loading the alphabetically-arranged mutants with military speed and precision. Two W. H. O. agents were positioned at the top of each loading ramp with one man calling out names from a list and the other stamping each mutant with an indelible number on the right shoulder and thigh.

I was standing, hands cuffed behind me, between the flashingly skinned green girl and a fat boy who had fingers growing out of the broad expanse of his naked stomach. They wiggled constantly. Though I had no heavier personal guard than any of the six hundred and eighty-seven (about one armed officer for every twenty chained mutants), when I stumbled once against the girl ahead, I saw at least ten guns instantly trained on me searching for some sign of hostility. I winked playfully at them.

The stamping process was not painless.

"Gylbre, Holly Martha," the list man called out.

We were directed to wait at the bottom of the ramp until our names were called, so it was a long walk up to the doorway, especially after seeing your fellows squirm and cry out while being stamped.

The Gylbre girl walked bravely up the plank and stopped at its top.

"Holly Gylbre?" the man asked.

"Yes," she whispered.

"Eighteen, 556 Almata Lane?"

"Y-yes."

The man checked the list on the stand at his side and stepped forward to firmly grasp her. "Okay, Wayne," he said.

The other man raised the stamp and pressed it roughly to her shoulder. At first, she involuntarily pulled away, but then she stiffened and, though I couldn't see her face, I could tell she was setting her jaw against the pain. After what seemed like a long time, the second man removed the stamp, leaving a clear "V118-53801" printed longwise in black letters on her arm. She visibly shuttered and started to step away.

"Hold it, babe," said the second man as he reset the stamp. "One more to go."

"Oh no! Do you *have* to?"

"Honey," he answered, "I *like* to."

She cried this time, quietly, as he pressed the stamp harshly into her thigh.

"Now," grinned the man as he slapped her sharply on the rump, "run along and admire your new tattoos."

As she stumbled into the shuttle's dark interior, the list man consulted his sheet. "Harper, Elias Blaine," he called out.

I strolled up the ramp with a rapidly spreading sneer on my lips and stopped between the two when the first man pushed lightly on my chest.

Smiling to expose my sharp teeth, I said, "Better watch it, we're contagious, you know."

He withdrew his hand with forced casualness and unconsciously wiped it on his trousers.

His partner, a really bright guy, laughed at his reaction. "S'matter, Davis? You didn't mind holding that little bit before this one, did you? Felt almost human, where I grabbed her, anyway."

I turned to him. "Class, buddy, solid class. I'll bet you finished your correspondence course from charm school at least a week before anyone else."

He stopped grinning, and his features darkened. "No talking in the ranks, freako," he spat while he set the stamp.

"I just figured that someone ought to lift the conversation above the level of dining apes. Did rather well, don't you think?"

"You think this is just a stamp to mark you for accounting, right?" The frown hardened. "Well, for some reason, it also contains thirty-five separate inoculations against any dangerous disease you might bring along on this little junket. Personally, I wouldn't give a tinker's damn if one of you misfits smuggled an old fashioned case of smallpox over there and wiped out the stinking place."

"I'll bet," I interrupted.

"You know, this is lined up so that the individual needles fit smoothly into a vein, but if I accidentally slipped up and positioned it wrong, it might just punch into some nerves."

"Really? And I might just faint from the pain and throw up all over your pretty uniform. Come to think of it, it *would* improve the smell around this place." I wrinkled my nose in obvious disgust.

Uttering a curse having to do with my immediate heritage, he slapped the stamp against my shoulder, ignored the thick black hair, and pressed. In a roundabout way, that was what I had wanted him to do. My pain threshold was fairly high, and I wanted to stare him in the eyes as he tried to intimidate me along with the other poor, scared kids he had already worked on that afternoon. The stamp did sting like a hive of angry bees, but I managed to keep my gaze from wavering.

"How'd you like that?" he asked uncertainly as he removed the stamp. Barely visible in black against the hair, "V118-53802" appeared. I had probably missed any of the beneficial effects of the inoculations, but that hardly mattered since, in all of my life, I had never been sick over four hours at a time. Another re   ., my mutated genes.

"Hmm?" I asked disinterestedly. "Oh, go ahead any time you're ready."

That shook him; he was used to reducing his victims to blubbering masses with slightly off-center shots like that one.

"Come on, Wayne," his partner prompted. "You're holding up the line."

Wayne applied the thigh stamp in a more regulation fashion, which was a good deal less painful, and gave me a push into the ship. "Keep up the good work, Wayne," I called back. "You'll make apprentice meat-cutter, yet."

Inside, another of the seemingly numberless guards personally showed me to my reclining liftoff couch, uncuffed my hands, and strapped me in. I rubbed a little circulation back into my wrists and lay gratefully back into the seat, closing my eyes.

"That really hurt, didn't it?" said the voice of Holly Gylbre at my left ear.

"Um hmm," I nodded, eyes remaining closed.

"But a lot of things are going to be rough from now on, I suppose."

"Hmm."

Her tone was subdued, afraid of rejection, but eager. "My name's Holly..."

"I know," I answered before she could finish. "I heard."

"Oh."

I heard and scented the fat boy with the fingers being strapped in on my right side.

"That, um, sort of puts me at a disadvantage, doesn't it?" she continued hopefully.

"You bet."

I thought that if I kept my eyes closed and yawned enough, she might take the hint. For reasons I didn't want to admit to myself, conversation with this girl was not the most desirable state of events in the world. That feeling bothered me even more.

"I once read that in pre-Plague times, there were some very primitive tribes in . . . Africa, I think, or maybe American Indians, well, anyway, they believe that if you knew a person's name and that person didn't know *your* name, then you had some sort of magical power over them."

"Abracadabra," I said.

Changing the subject, she sighed breathfully. "This loading may take some time longer, and there's nothing much to do."

"I plan to take a short nap to be ready for my first space flight."

"That's probably a good idea. After all, Capella's pretty far away . . ."

"Forty-five light years," I said.

"You really don't want to talk to me, do you?" she asked.

"Very perceptive," I replied.

"Why?"

Why? Because of the uneasiness I had felt since first being surrounded by people like Jeff and Holly Gylbre? Because of what I had more recently developed into? Because I was afraid to face the fact of my own irrational bigotry? "You're a freak," I said.

Pain and anger sprang into her voice. "And you're too good to talk to 'freaks'? Just-just because of my skin . . . I wasn't . . . well, d-damn it, you're a freak yourself!"

"Nope," I disagreed.

"You're not?"

"Right. I'm an official agent of W. H. O.'s special deportation operations. I'm here to check on how the treatment of exiled mutants is in actuality, contrasting with how it is reported."

"But . . . you look like one!"

"Special effects."

She believed it, I thought guiltily, and why not? She had been ripped from her home life and thrust into a chaotic world beyond her range of experience. Come on, Eli, what are *you* becoming?

I opened my eyes and faced her. That smooth, apparently poreless green face topped by long, shockingly blond hair looked back at me. Her face read, respectively, surprise, confusion, and comprehension. "Hey, you're just joking!"

"Right."

Liftoff was one of the most frightening and magnificent

occurrences in my life up until that time. Though I didn't lose consciousness, I felt as if I was being flattened by some invisible blanket as the little shuttlecraft struggled to reach the breakaway velocity from the world's viciously powerful gravity. I had wondered if I would scream, but was surprised to find that the only sound emitted by any of the seventy passengers was a low, dull groan that fogged into silence.

Once we were definitely locked into our proper orbital path, eight or ten of the weaker stomached among us suddenly developed severe cases of nausea. We had been issued plastic stocking bags for just such emergencies, and some of them were utilized, but at least one mutant didn't have time. In the absence of normal gravity (which could have been produced by centrifugal force), the splattering cloud of "undesirable material" writhed, divided, and coiled upon itself.

"Oh, hell," came the pilot's voice from the compartment before us. "I told you people to keep those blamed bags close to your mouths! Geller, man the pump!"

I chuckled silently as Geller, a youngish, wormish man, floated into the passenger area guiding a large cannister to which was connected a long, white suction hose. Locking himself magnetically to the inner hull of the ship, he still performed some hilarious aerial acrobatics in tracking down the expanding goo.

"Kind of scary," Holly stated, breathing heavily.

"I suppose so."

To my disappointment, there were no portholes or visiplates in the hull to show us the black majesty that we were speeding through. I had really wanted to see the colossal interstellar barge that was scheduled to make this journey of almost inconceivable distance, but after no more than fifteen minutes of careful maneuvering, we docked with no more than a gentle bump.

"Okay," said the pilot over the audio system, "everybody remain seated and strapped in. When we're completely sealed up, some of the men will come back and lead you one at a time, repeat, one at a time out of the shuttle into the main ship."

No one made the transfer between ships with any sort of grace or speed, since we were practically pulled through the air by magnetically booted crewmen. I compared the experience to being dragged across the calm surface of a lake or sliding down a smooth ramp in a cotton-padded suit. We had another couple of queasy stomachs, but nothing so bad as previously.

"I wonder where our rooms are?" asked a boy about twelve

inches high to his companion, who looked like a two-foot lizard.

"Stay in line, stay in line!" an armed guard yelled as we milled (or drifted) around in the immense receiving cabin of the barge. "I keep tellin' 'em to tie you stupid bastards in line. Gvaldi, Simon G., I need Simon Gvaldi over here!"

A man disentangled himself from the mass and, pulling along the vertical standards projecting up from the floor, arrived at the spot. "Gvaldi, sir," he responded.

"Simon G.? Good. You stay right here," said the guard. Then, raising his voice, he continued, "Gvaldi, Wilma Jane! Over here! Gwella, Matthew! No, no, you midgets have got special cabinets in section three! Three, yeah! Gwenn, Eileen, good. Gylbre, Holly M.! Gylbre!"

Holly made her way to the man, and I followed, figuring to be next. Sure enough, there were no Hackles, Hadleys, Hannahs, or Harmons, and "Harper, Elias B.!" was the guard's next call.

As we were sorted, we were led through a short hall into a long, cylindrical room containing row on row of four-by-seven foot metal boxes. A quick representative count gave me an estimate of one hundred fifty. They looked like chrome colored coffins and reminded me of tales of cleaning up after the Plague.

"All right," said our guard, "remember your places in line, then females to the right, males to the left, empty your bowels and bladders and get back. You've got ten minutes."

Someone spoke up in a confused voice, "What's this all about?"

"Kid, this is the last time you'll get the opportunity before we hit Capella, now move some tails!"

Not particularly eager to test the truth behind his claim, I moved. Back in the room, we were lined up in front of the boxes and, on command, lay down in their cushioned interiors. The illusion of a coffin was reinforced as the sides of the box cut off any other view than the sides and the ceiling.

The guard continued to call out instructions, "To the right of your head you'll find a face mask recessed into the side of the compartment. Pull it out and fasten it to your nose and mouth, snugly, but not tightly enough to be uncomfortable." I did. "Now, fit the back of your head into the depression below it so that your neck lies on a plane with the rest of your body. Place your arms at your sides, palms flat, and straighten your legs."

Then I knew. Damn, I thought, I wonder if I'll ever see space from the inside.

"Okay, Numata," the guard said. "Close and spray."

From the wall above the top of my head, a clear plastic slab lowered over the top of the box and snapped shut with a solid click. A squirt of something cold rushed out of the mask to cover my face. I tried to blink, but my eyes only got halfway (closed) before sleep overtook me.

2

"In the Land of My Own Kind!"

My entire time upon the starship, approximately seven months one way, is no more than twenty minutes of memories. Though I awoke slowly over a period of hours, my rousing was a thing of partiality. I would feel the needles that periodically jabbed revitalizing fluids into my body and then drift quietly into twilight until the next shot. I didn't fully awaken until the same guard of seven months before flipped open the lid and dug roughly at my ribs.

"Get out," he grunted. "You're home."

A single defined and penetrating thought interrupted my dazed consciousness: I had to go to the bathroom. It was a common sentiment as all one hundred and fifty of us struggled in uncoordinated weightlessness for relief. Surprisingly, some of us made it.

I was in a group of seventy that was called to a shuttlecraft immediately afterward. We were all hungry, sore, disoriented, but the cumulative effect of our protests was exactly nil, and the guns were all loosened to insure our compliance.

"Listen, joker," said one guard, responding to a complaint, "while you were frozen down, you aged exactly twelve hours. You're *not* going to starve to death before landfall, okay?"

Sure, I thought while being strapped in next to Holly, there will be a reception center at the farms below with hot meals and cool water. They don't get seven hundred new arrivals every day of the week.

This, one of the first pleasant expectations I had entertained since being tracked down a few days (or seven months) previously, lightened my battered spirits as we blasted away from the main ship

31

and spiralled down to the large green globe below. The landfall was a hundred per cent easier than the liftoff, despite doing some tricky things to my confused inner ear, and almost before we realized we were settling gently to earth, or a close approximation of it.

"Now to be greeted by the cheering throngs," someone commented. We began to fumble with the seat straps.

"Remain seated!" came the familiar voice of the pilot. "Everyone remain in your seat; you will be escorted out in preselected numbers."

"Probably a plan to slowly reaccustom us to gravity," I explained to Holly's perplexed look. I like to sound confidently authoritative whenever I have the guts.

A crewman holding the loading sheet appeared at the cabin door, hesitated, and called back to the pilot compartment, "Hey, how many do we unload in each section?"

The now easily recognizable pilot's voice replied, "Computer says any number over twenty-two point seven is risking a reaction."

"Twenty-two, then?"

"Suits me."

"Okay." The man with the list turned back to us. "Starting with the back row next to the door, sound by number, last name, first name. Start."

From behind me and to my right, a timid voice said, "One, uh, Jonovitch, Mahail."

"Unstrap. Next!"

"Two, Jonan, Hector."

"Unstrap. Next!"

This ran back up through the J's and into the I's before number twenty-two shouted out. I calmly rationalized the process as a distribution among the various farms, such as I and most other Earth inhabitants had seen many times in W. H. O. documentaries about Thear. It was only when the hatch opened to release the chosen number that we could see outside into this new world.

No farms, no greeting natives, no rolling meadows. Only a heavy green jungle.

The twenty-two were swiftly hustled out and ears not as sharp as mine probably didn't hear the startled comments of the mutants or the crisp replies of the guards.

Where were the promised plantations? This wasn't Thear!

This *was* Thear! The real Thear, your home for the rest of your natural lives. Now spread into the protective jungle.

Inside the shuttle, the remaining forty-eight of us set up a low, puzzled hum, unable in the most part to make out the muffled words of those outside.

Holly looked at me with her dark green gaze and asked, "What are they doing out there? Why can't the rest of us leave?"

Just beginning to understand, I slowly shook my head. "Little girl," I said, "we have been royally shafted."

So, in groups of twenty-two, we were abandoned. After letting the first perplexed souls wander aimlessly into the surrounding wilderness, the ship lifted a safe "seventeen point oh five" miles to the west before setting down again, where the next twenty-two were herded off. They understood little more than their predecessors, and most were even surprised once again to fail to find the expected Earth civilization carved out of the trees and underbrush. I debated spreading the news that I had overheard on the first landing, but looking at the ever-tense guards convinced me that any form of resistance could only result in a massacre—ours, of course.

Seventeen point oh five miles to the northwest, the third group of frightened and betrayed mutants were forced off of the ship at gunpoint and left to their fate. The checklist man had wanted to unload the last four of us with this number, but the pilot refused to allow any more than twenty-two point seven to depart at any one landing site. None of us volunteered to be that point seven of a person, and a fourth and final landing to dispose of the remainder was necessary.

Naturally enough, we all knew what lay in store for us, and the prospect of untamed wilderness in the place of storybook communes did little to settle our nerves. The boy with the fingers—Harriman was his name—couldn't take the pressure; tearing himself free of his seat straps while we were in flight, he began screaming at the astonished guards and even made an abortive attack on one. Another subdued him before he crossed the cabin.

"That does it!" called the checklist man. "Break out the cuffs, Shozo."

"Cuffs? Hell, Bert there's only *four* of them," the man answered.

"I don't care if there is only one! You can't trust these freaks; they're all right on the line of craziness, and I've seen what these . . . these *animals* will do! Cuff 'em up, behind their backs!"

I whistled aloud. "Oh, man, you can't be serious. You have guns, you know, to kill us with. Me, I prefer another forty-five, fifty years down there over a bullet in my brain. Now, if you're offering a two week cruise . . ."

"Crazy!" the checklist man declared. "Didn't I tell you?"

Another guard produced four sets of handcuffs, and we were instantly stood on our feet and locked up. They were none too considerate in the process.

We remained standing throughout the landing, but this caused no difficulties, since the ability and experience of the pilot made our touchdown little more than a step from a curb. The head man made an absolutely superfluous check of his list and, along with an insurance guard, rushed us off the shuttle. Harriman was breaking down.

The sun (or suns, since Capella is a tight binary), after seven months of interstellar travel, was both a welcome and painful change. On the edge of a bountiful green growth, we breathed the unprocessed air of an open world, shook free the collected kinks and strains, and stepped carefully in our bare feet on the long, gray-green grass.

"You people just split up, now," said the checklist man in obvious relief at having his duty performed for this trip. "Run along like good little gawfs, so we can get the hell out of here."

Harriman was practically screaming through tears when he begged, "Don't leave us, please, oh God, don't leave us here, please!"

The two men looked at one another and broke out in laughter.

"We'll die! I know it!" the sobbing boy continued. "If you won't take us all, take me, please . . ."

Checklist man answered him, "Listen, freak, unless you want to get fried by our exhaust, you'd better take my advice and haul ass."

Harriman fell to his knees, crying.

The girl who made up the fourth member of our group coughed suggestively, "Aren't you fellows forgetting something? I like to wear my bracelets on one wrist at a time, if you don't mind."

The second guard spoke while staring at her toeless feet. "Well, miss, the performance of your friend here has induced us to leave behind a little token of our visit. Maybe in a year or two, they'll rust off."

"You can't!" a wide-eyed Holly exclaimed. "You can't leave us like *this*!"

"Just watch, sugar, just watch." The guard pointed his gun at the space of ground separating us from the ship. "Now, scat!" He fired a shot into the earth.

At the explosion, the two girls leaped back, but Harriman remained where he sat with head bowed.

"I said move, fatso!" the guard repeated. He placed a shot right next to Harriman's knees, but the boy sat as motionless as a statue. "I'll blow your damned head off!"

As he aimed again, I said in a low, even voice, "Leave him alone." In reply, he shot the dirt between my feet, which shattered a stone that sprayed my ankles.

"Now, whaddya say, comedian?"

I paused before answering, "I *wish* you wouldn't do that."

That was when I should have turned tail and run, just as my natural sense of logic, and more importantly innate cowardice, begged me to do, but the hate was boiling in my brain by then. Instead of running, I walked toward him.

The smirk was still there when he shot the next bullet at my feet, but it disappeared in shock when my right foot flashed out and knocked his weapon fifty feet through the air. All of his expressions vanished under a mask of blood as I continued my quick turn and caught his left cheek with the heel of my left foot. He dropped like a pole-axed steer.

The list man made some furtive move toward his own gun, but I stopped that by screaming as much like an animal as I was able and leaping some eight feet straight up. He dropped his clipboard and sprinted into the ship.

"Eli," Holly marvelled.

Tensing my shoulders, I snapped the cuffs, picked up the unconscious form of the guard, and tossed him into the ship just as the hatch hummed shut. I was cursing with words I'd never had the time or opportunity to use when the long, revolving barrel of a high caliber rapid fire gun extended from its cubbyhole and began spitting a continuous stream of metal at us. I lost all of my righteous indignation and raced for cover, as did the girls, but I saw Harriman, unhurt and conscious, lying where he had fallen.

So? He wasn't my responsibility, and his sniveling pleas hadn't inspired my attack in the first place. The guy had two legs; he could save himself.

I was more intent on dodging the bullets, since the man at the trigger seemed to have given the girls only stimulating misses and concentrated his legitimate anger on my posterior. From necessity, I ignored the briars and thorns that dug into my legs and feet as I blundered my way through the clinging underbrush into the safety of the forest. A bullet missing your ear by the width of a hen's tooth can make a person ignore a lot of minor pains.

Like an air bubble breaking the surface of a stagnant pool, I suddenly burst through the brush into the comparative openness of the forest below the treetops, and, just as I clutched at a cooling and badly needed breath, the shuttle lifted. The backwash of the rockets—fired, I'm sure, with intentional vehemence—rolled from the clearing, through the brush, and caught me when I wasn't looking in its hot grip.

I was tossed in the air like a gumwrapper in a gale, spinning violently before hitting the ground and immediately shifting into another unscheduled sleep.

The light wasn't really emerald, more of a red-speckled hazel. I reached this monumental conclusion while lying flat on my back and staring lazily up at the nearly unbroken canopy of leaf-laden trees. I had just awakened from a nap of indeterminate duration and, apart from a dull pain in the back of my head, felt none the worse for the experience.

The trees seemed to rise from the earth a good twenty feet from one another and stood an average of about sixty feet. They had few substantial branches for three quarters of their height, but suddenly burst out like giant mushrooms above that. The thick limbs grew intertwining with one another, forming a ceiling that left little space for young saplings to elbow their way to the sun.

The lack of sunlight filtering down from the canopy caused the forest floor to be very bare apart from a densely soft carpet of dead leaves, brown in their decay. I figured that the trees themselves probably went through a stage similar to Earth's funguses when they were independent of sunlight in early growth, though I wondered if any type of fungus could grow to such great size and form a bark-like outer covering.

"You know, you can't lie here forever," I sagely informed myself. "Got to check for broken bones eventually and decide how seriously this revolting turn of developments will affect your career as a despotic playboy."

I was a little more solemn as I tentatively moved each section of my person, always expecting the keen stab of pain that would inform me of important injury. Nothing but my head seemed to be rebellious.

"So," I continued my intensely interesting one-man conversation, "get up."

I did, wobbling a bit at first, but regaining my composure quickly enough. Leaning against a thick tree, I picked at the embedded thorns in my feet and legs until it was safe to stand again. I had wondered exactly how I would react when the full impact of being abandoned on another world hit me, and right then I found out: I was hungry.

Seven months is about the record for a fast on my part, and I had no intentions of trying for eight, so, even though I had no knowledge of what was edible on this planet, I went foraging. Maybe they had some fruit high in the branches, but I elected to continue my search on the ground before venturing to that altitude.

The animals began to make their appearances. All of the W. H. O.-produced documentaries concerning Earth B had focused almost entirely on the communal agricultural society so benevolently overseen by Kurtz' personal appointees. This meant that few outside of the elite scientific hierarchy knew any details of the natural lifeforms of the planet. Like any other uninformed inhabitant of Earth, I took it for granted that Thear contained your average fauna setup: sea animals, insects, land animals, and fowls, with the more advanced mammals dominating. A few minutes of strolling through the forest changed this attitude.

I saw a beetle (?) that was at least thirty inches long attacked by a blue lizard half its size, the latter barely able to crawl away on its distended belly. I watched as a bat-like creature became disturbed by my passing and leaped into the air to fly directly into a tree trunk, apparently blinded by the dim, treecut daylight. A kind of snake with umbrella-like frills behind its head slithered quickly from under my right foot as I jumped back. Since I didn't know what to be afraid of, I retained a certain amount of caution toward everything.

I didn't see anything bulkier than the beetle, but I figured this was because of the time of day and the fact that this part of the land offered little food for animals other than termites. The suns seemed to be sliding down in what I took to be the west before I stumbled out into a wide clearing centered by a good-sized stream of clear water. It could, of course, be poison to my foreign system, but, conversely, I could also starve or die of thirst. I hardly paused before plunging my head and then the rest of me into it.

Other than a slight sulphur flavor, the water tasted like good old H2O and was cool and free of dirt or organisms that I could detect. A convulsive tremor took hold of me, and I realized how tired, scared, and tense I really had become over what seemed to be the last few days. Only four of my days ago, I had been a normal member of Kurtz' "New Born Humanity," a working, structured inhabitant of an Earth that was just beginning to drag itself from the most terrible ordeal of recorded existence.

I felt seventy-five to eighty per cent better when I dragged myself onto a large, slate-like rock to dry. A couple of bushes grew nearby, and each sprouted a different type of fruit, one long and yellow like a banana, and the other green and round. Without having to rise, I plucked the first and dug out a portion with my thumbnail. I also gagged and spat out the piece when its sharp, acidic taste bit my gums and tongue.

"Jeeze," I gasped, "I'll have to do better than *that*!"

And I did with the second choice. It reminded me a little of a big olive with plenty of juice and no pimento. Two or three others gave me a pleasant bulging šensation, and I lay back contentedly, eyes closed. All at once, the sun was down, and the forest was audibly alive.

Sleep fled. The croåkings, twitters, rumbles, and squeals washed my feeling of complacency away like a bucket of water in the face, as I lay there in the star-punctured darkness. Come on, I told myself, you're not going to let some noises scare you, are you?

Something small and cold landed on my chest and leaped into the stream.

Damned rock was too hard, anyway.

High in the uncomfortable, but safe bole of a tree, I spent my first night on Thear. Below me, I heard strange noises from large and small animals congregating to drink before setting out on another hard night of hunting and being hunted. Though I couldn't see any of the animals, my imagination provided plenty of threatening bodies for the growls and grunts.

Once, toward dawn, I thought I heard human voices.

My first daybreak on Thear broke without me. Only occasionally dozing during the night proper (which, I remembered with regret, would last around fifteen hours), I finally slipped off into deep sleep just as the eastern sky was going from black to purple, and I didn't wake until at least six hours later.

Despite the insistence of my stomach and protests of my mistreated back, I was awakened by a sound below me, from the direction of the stream. It was a splashing noise, punctuated by short, high cries. Trying to remain quiet and unnoticed, I rolled over and looked down.

She was having a lot of trouble just getting a drink of water for breakfast because her hands were still cuffed behind her. Holly Gylbre was afraid to go too deeply into the slippery mud, knowing that if she fell the odds of recovering her feet wouldn't be the greatest in the world, and, for the same reason, she couldn't bend over too far. Her long blond hair was stringing wet, and most of the water she had managed to reach was on her face.

Finally getting her fill (or coming up for air), she half-fell onto the bank and sat on the same rock I had stretched out upon the night before. She was nice looking, I decided, though small, and that skin gave her a coated-in-plastic shininess that was rather unsettling. Of the hundreds of thousands of mutants exported to this planet, I should probably be able to do better than Holly.

It hit me again, the true roots of this disdain for her and all the rest I'd been thrown in with. It was bigotry, "normal human superiority" drilled into me, not by my parents, who couldn't afford the vice, but by my childhood friends and teachers. Mutants were less than we were, more bestial, not as important. And the Kurtz dogma of "God's Blueprint."

Here I sat, fifty feet above the ground in a tree, my arms and shoulders carpeted in short, thick hair, my teeth sharp and strong, and I still retained some of that old biased crap.

"Hey," I called down to her, "had breakfast, yet?"

She heard and looked around quickly, but was unable to locate me.

"Up here, in the tree!"

"Eli?" she called back uncertainly.

"Right. Over here."

She found me and smiled. "I thought you were dead! When the rocket blasted off and it knocked you through the air like that . . . I thought it killed you!"

"Scared me half to death, but it'll take more than that to kill me." Saying this, I decided to test my theory. All of my life, I had been admonished not to show any difference in myself at school or at play, and, because of this, I really didn't know exactly of what I was capable.

I looked at the ground. Fifty feet vertical is a lot longer than fifty feet horizontal, and I wasn't so sure I should start out on such an ambitious note, but, what the hell, even if I broke a couple of bones, they'd knit in a matter of hours. Before I had time to think and allow my natural cowardice to talk some reason into me, I swung out on a branch and dropped.

I hit the cushiony grass on all fours and went immediately into a roll to negate the shock. No breaks, not even a sprain! When I stopped rolling, I was next to Holly. Looking up, I repeated, "Had breakfast, yet?"

A little startled by my style of descending the tree, it took her a moment for the words to sink in. "What? Oh, no, I-I haven't been able to eat anything, yet, because of my hands. And I really am hungry."

"These green things here are okay to eat," I said, selecting one, "at least, they haven't killed me since last night." I bit deeply into my prize.

The hunger spilled from her eyes as she watched. "Do you think . . . I mean, I saw how you did . . . could you help me get out of these?" Holly asked, cocking her head to indicate the handcuffs.

"You don't like them?" I asked in mock surprise. "The wrong color, perhaps? Well, I do agree that they would go better in the front. Turn around."

I stuck the rest of the huge olives between my teeth and took hold of the cuffs. The chain wasn't very big, since most prisoners could hardly have broken it with such awful leverage, and I snapped it, leaving only the bracelets around her wrists.

"Oh, thanks!" she breathed in relief. "I was practically helpless like that. If any animal of any size had come along while—well, thanks a lot."

"Don't mention it. Give me your hand." Taking it, I positioned the metal ring against the rock, held it with my left hand, and struck it sharply with the heel of my right. Just like it had the night before for me, the blow sprang the lock mechanism and it popped open. A similar operation on her other hand completed the task. "I'll put that on your bill. Where are the others?"

She was still massaging her wrists when she replied, "The girl and boy? I don't know. The blastoff sort of stunned me, and when I came around, the girl was gone."

"And the boy?"

"He wouldn't move, even when they were shooting."

"You mean he actually stayed in the *clearing*?"

She nodded. "He just sat there, crying, and the rockets . . ." her voice broke into a whisper, "they burned him up."

I sighed. "Now, *that's* stupid!"

"I guess he just couldn't face living here."

"A-One Dumb. It's no skin off my nose, though. Have an olive."

Holly ate greedily for a time, pausing to talk aimlessly about a variety of subjects as she did. "I was normal, really, until last year. Then my skin began to blotch like this, at first on my legs. When it was only in spots, I could cover it with makeup and the right clothes, but, a couple of months ago—I mean, a couple of months before we were launched for here, it kind of exploded. In three days, I was ... like this all over."

"And the troops caught you," I supplied, tossing away a black seed as long as the last joint in my thumb.

"Well, no. I wanted to go out West, to Washington, and live in one of those abandoned cities, you know? But Mom and Daddy explained how it would be better for all concerned if I—"

"Your *parents* turned you in?" I asked in disbelief.

"They explained it to me first, about being with my own kind—"

"Your own parents? I can't believe it! It's their fault you're a freak in the first place!"

"But Director Kurtz has shown how it's best to separate real people from—"

"Bullshit! That half-witted numbskull has brainwashed the entire population of Earth with his 'peaceful haven for mutants' bit. He's turned our own families against us! Boy, your folks must have just waited for some excuse to get rid of you."

"No, that's not true! You don't even know them; what gives you the right to talk like that? Who turned *you* in?"

I laughed grimly. "My best friend, right after I saved his life. Listen, I'm sorry about what I said, okay? Let's just drop the subject."

We sat there in silence, while a steady breeze rolled over us.

"So," she finally said, "there aren't really any farms?"

"Looks that way."

"What do we do now?"

I studied a blade of grayish grass intensely before answering. "Try to survive, I guess. Find a cave or something to live in, get some meat and vegetables to supplement our diet. Maybe we'll get lucky and find some more of those thousands abandoned here through the years."

A sudden memory lit her face. "There are some more people here! Last night, I hid in a thicket and some of them passed right next to me, talking."

"Sure it wasn't that other girl who came with us?"

"It couldn't have been. There were at least two of them, and their voices were too deep for girls. I stayed hidden because of the way I was, you know?"

I looked at a movement a few hundred yards down the riverbank. "How many would you guess there were?"

"I don't really know. Maybe five."

"Maybe, here come three of them right now."

Three tall, white men were strolling slowly up the stream toward us. They all carried spears with wooden shafts and stone heads, and two of them were dressed in animal hides, while the third still had his W. H. O.-issued trunks. One was old enough to sport a full beard.

"Do you think they're mutants?" Holly whispered.

"Yeah, look at that last guy's face and arms; he looks like a gargoyle from some old cathedral."

"You want to . . . meet them?"

"On my terms. I don't like the looks of those spears." I stood and tugged on her arm. "Let's fade into the underbrush for a time."

We had crept halfway to the comparative safety of the trees when a tall, skinny boy with a body like rubber dough stepped out before us. "Ah, leaving so soon? And we were just beginning to enjoy this tender scene." He waved over his shoulder and eleven other mutants of varying degrees of grotesqueness appeared from the forest to join him.

"I really must be slipping," I sighed as they surrounded us.

While their three fellows trudged upstream to join them, the tall boy began to explain. "You must be new arrivals to our little world. How do you like it so far?"

"Oh, terrific," I said, stalling. "As cosy as any jungle I've ever had the privilege to be marooned in. The flies and snakes are truly authentic-looking."

"We're the Berserkers, the most powerful tribe on the whole damned planet, and you two are passing through our territory without official authorization. If you'd like to keep your brains and features about you, I suggest you do your utmost to please our esteemed leader, Sir Kammon." He bowed and stepped aside for a squat, muscular white man with scales covering his upper body in a natural armor.

Sir Kammon walked slowly around the two of us, lending one yellowish eye to inspection. He stopped in front of Holly and plucked her lower lip with a forefinger. In a raw, injured voice, he growled, "Is this yours?"

"Holly? No, not mine," I answered with wide-eyed innocence. At least half of them were carrying stone spears or knives, and at fifteen to two, I didn't like the odds.

"She don't own you, does she? I heard of perversion like that up north aways."

"No, we're just a couple of wayfaring wanderers who didn't

know we were wayfaring in your territory. No harm intended, believe me." My motto is: if you can talk your way out of a fight, do.

"I like her," Kammon went on. He slid one finger down her cheek and neck, obviously enjoying the sensation and squealing noise the action caused. "I like the way she sounds. That's a switch, a rubber covered girl!" He laughed, and, as if cued, so did all of his men. They all stopped abruptly. "You know, you owe me for the use of my stream and the fruit you ate. How much you askin' for her?"

Holly shot a panicked look at me and I shrugged. "Like I said, I've got no property rights to her."

"Then, what do you have to offer?"

"Uh...a quick song and dance?"

They broke into laughter again. "You'd demean yourself like that just to keep from getting stomped?" Kammon demanded with a huge grin.

"Damn right," I replied.

"Well, I'm afraid that won't do. This little baby doll here," he squeezed one of Holly's breasts, bringing a short cry from her, "is already mine, or I should say, ours. But you are still in debt, son."

I *definitely* didn't like the odds. "I suppose that means you're not going to let me slink away in silence, tail between my legs."

"Right," he said, obscenely dragging out the word.

"Le's stomp him!" a husky six-footer roared. The rest chorused their assent.

"Hold it, hold it, good knights of the Berserkers," Kammon shouted. "Let's allow Sir Brownley decide this one. He hasn't had a voice in weeks."

The slim boy who had first spoken to us smiled devilishly. "Well, sirs, the way I see it, this interloper has got three alternatives."

Holly started to protest, but Kammon absently slapped her quiet.

"What are these, uh, alternatives?" I asked.

Brownley continued to grin. "One, you can pass out or break and run."

"That sounds reasonable," I muttered.

"Two, you can kiss our butts and submit to a life of slavery."

"That doesn't sound so reasonable."

"And thirdly, you have the option of whipping all fifteen of us and walking away scott free."

"Hmm," I hmm'd, wiping my palms on my thighs. "I guess that leaves me only one choice." I held up my fists in a fighter's stance.

A growling cheer rumbled from the men, and they dropped their lances to the ground. This could be handled with hands, feet, and knees.

"Man, you are in-sane," proclaimed Kammon. He pulled Holly to one side and shouted, "Berserkers, rampage!"

Hardened and wise in the ways of dirty fighting, they charged me in roughly intentional packs. If I was going to have any chance whatsoever against fourteen attackers, speed and surprise were necessities, so I waited in a fixed position until the first boy was practically slobbering in my face. At the last second, I sidestepped and caught in the pit of his back with my right elbow, which sent him headfirst into the stream. The man just behind him suddenly found my left foot in his stomach. A third Berserker caught the back of my left fist with his teeth. He dropped.

The others hung back momentarily after the failure of the first assault. Three of their number were down, one unconscious, and the rest began to rethink their decision considering weapons. My reactions were quicker than theirs, and my frame housed a strength not revealed by my outer appearance.

With an explosive scream, the biggest of their number leaped into the air and rushed me. I ducked his wild grab and landed a short right to his face, feeling his jaw crunch under my knuckles. He fell out, but the man from the stream landed on my back, trying to ride me to the bank. I shook him off the way he came and took the initiative. Too soon, I knew, they would realize that the way to beat me was to bodily force me to the ground where my mobility and reflexes would be hampered, so I rammed my shoulder into the foremost of the group and sent three of them down. A knotted fist smashed against my cheek, sending globes of light spinning under my eyelids, but it didn't stagger me, and I managed to kick him behind the left ear. Picking up a fallen body, I threw the man into a mass of Berserkers as a diversionary tactic while I planned my next offensive.

One boy swung a long, heavy club at my head, and though I was able to catch and break it before it connected, my own attention was diverted.

"Eli!" I heard Holly scream. And, stupidly, I turned.

Somebody's knee smashed up into my crotch with savage force, and my entire body was instantly on fire. Choking, I tumbled to the ground.

Feet were suddenly in my ribs and stomach, landing again and again while I writhed, but I had enough steam left to lash out in a wide arc at the tens of legs surrounding me. A kind of cold humor covered me, as my body began to numb to the blows; I knew I'd cracked at least three legs on the last swipe.

My last positive action was to clutch an ankle that had been descending on my throat and crush it.

Consciousness weaved in my brain like a drunk after a good bottle of wine, sometimes here, sometimes there. In my more rational moments, I realized that I was no longer at the mercy of the knightly Berserkers, but was being carried along on some sort of stretcher, and the ride was none too smooth. My mouth periodically filled with bitter fluid that I spat to one side to help my breathing.

"Didn't make my option," I muttered through the haze of pain.

"What'd he say?" one of my unknown bearers asked.

"I dunno. He's whacked out. Let's get him over to Joanna's hut before he croaks," the second answered.

"Where's the birdy?"

"She's being 'assisted' to the village by Finnegan, where else?"

The first voice laughed. "Where else, indeed?"

I faded away.

3

"The Tribes of Thear"

I recovered consciousness inside a little fire-lit hut. In my mind, I was in the rich, green meadows, waiting, and the pipes were playing.

"Joanna!" came a voice through my insulating cloud. "He's awake, Joanna! You're going to be all right," the voice, a girl's, assured me.

"You're just saying that," I laughed.

"Oh, Eli, I thought you were going to die!"

"No confidence," I clucked at her, "no confidence."

"Out of the way, honey," a new girl's voice urged her. "The lug seems to have hung on." Hands suddenly began to do things to my body in an expert fashion. I found my head propped up and a hot, tasty liquid forced between my lips.

"Chicken soup?" I asked.

"Close enough. Drink it, dummy. It can't do any good on the outside."

"Yes, ma'am." With awe-inspiring effort, I pried my eyelids open to look glassily up at the girl ministering to my wounds. She had short, painfully purple hair, long, purple whiskers, three working eyes, and the biggest mouth I'd seen outside of a fish. "You, my dear, are the second ugliest girl I've ever met."

She dropped my head to the packed ground and answered, "I like you, too, now shut up and get some rest."

And I would have, but a medium height, well-muscled black man of around twenty-two or three entered the hut just then. He was smiling and, strangely enough, his face looked like he grinned a lot. He was followed by a tall, lean man with bright red hair and a crooked nose, a shorter, brown-haired boy with two extra arms

46

below his regulation ones, and, bringing up the rear in truly admirable fashion, a tall, slender girl who was built as well as any six women I'd met back on Earth.

"Well, how do you do," I said to her, battling a swimming head and stomach to prop myself up on one elbow.

"Greetings," said the black man with the pointed ears and nose. He appeared to be their leader. "I'm Charles Garner, this dumb Irishman is Finnegan, this is Allen Starett, and the chick is Sheila Roen."

"Delighted all around," I said. "I suppose that makes me Elias B. Harper, lately of the planet Earth."

They nodded. Garner continued, "I think about half of this village lost a week of fresh kills on you, Mr. Elias Harper. We bet you wouldn't live. But, by God, you're knitted up just about."

The dull pains around my body didn't feel just about knitted up. "Gosh, that makes me feel guilty."

The tall Irishman with a fine, though short pair of horns sprouting over his temples laughed loudly. "Don't, man; anybody who can lay out nine of those damned Berserkers deserves to live a long life with all of the booze and broads he can handle. Hell, if you'd dodged that nut shot, I'll back even odds that you'd have wiped out the whole pack."

"It was a fine example of aggressive self-defense," Starett intoned in a scholarly voice, as he adjusted a well-cracked pair of thick-lensed glasses.

"Really?" I said. "Personally, I felt that I did a great job of getting the slop beaten out of me. How come my defeat is so well spread around here, wherever this happens to be?"

"Your girl told us about it," Garner said, pointing past my head to a dark corner of the hut. I bridged my neck enough to see Holly sitting quietly there, watching us. "She practically replayed the fight, blow by blow."

"Strange kid," Finnegan mumbled. "Wouldn't leave your side for the last two days."

"Two days?" I exploded, experiencing a time suspension shock for the second time in a matter of days. "They must have kicked me but good."

"They did," Garner agreed. "When we came by on a hunting, the six guys still standing were pounding you on the head, and one was using a stick."

"Yeah, but when we spooked 'em, they had nine bodies to drag off," Finnegan assured me.

"Makes me feel all warm inside," I replied. "Don't you have something to add about my glorious victory?" I asked Sheila.

"Let's just say I'd like to have you on my side," she purred.

Any time, I dreamed, any time. I looked gratefully at her softly rounded form, still finding none of the usual deformities. I learned later that she had no detectable variance and had passed her gene test, but had been exiled because she was the only child of two affected parents.

"So," I went on, "where do I stand in this situation, slave, hero, dogcatcher?"

Almost everyone found this to be hilarious.

A sober-faced Starett explained, "While there are many diverse socio-political 'tribes' disseminated throughout this continental mass, you were fortunate enough to be released in an area controlled—and I use the word in a liberal sense—by a loosely knit group of people who wish only to be allowed to live and govern our own actions in our separate manners. We are not communistic, since each individual or unit has to provide for himself, just as we are not democratic, since public opinion has no effect on the individual's decisions.

"We unite in rare instances, two of the more common being to hunt big game with some measure of safety and to defend our right to live in this form of society, if such it is."

"You mean I can live any way I want as long as it doesn't hurt anybody else?"

"Correct."

"Not in *my* home," stated Joanna, the girl who had cared for me while I was out. "As soon as you can walk, you and your little bedmate can seek your own pastures. And you look like you can walk right now."

"Don't worry," Garner smiled. "We've got some fairly dry caves down at the south end; you two can sleep there until you build your own place or move on."

Holly's voice was nervous and embarrassed from the dark corner, "We're not married. I mean, I just met him on the trip here."

I tossed Sheila a look, which she fielded with a casual smile.

"We don't get many preachers out this way," explained Finnegan. "Naturally, our standards have changed."

"Well, this is interesting," Joanna said, standing, "but I think the patient needs to get some food inside him and a little more sleep."

"Aw, you *are* worried about me."

"Shoot, I just don't want to have you around any longer than necessary," she replied.

"I'll just bet you that I'm up and out of here by this time tomorrow."

"It's a bet."

And I was, too.

I was shown around the camp the next afternoon by Allen Starett, the walking encyclopedia that everyone called Doc. Starett himself had been on Thear only two years, having been clever enough to hide his obvious physical variation under "fat clothes" for sixteen years of his life, and he had a sponge-like mind and a photographic memory that allowed him to absorb and retain thousands of useful and useless facts.

He was intrigued with the amazing speed with which my exterior wounds had closed to thin, pale scars, while my internal injuries had healed enough to allow me to walk around without pain. I tried to explain that quick regeneration was one of the more bearable facets of my variance, but he continued to quietly shake his head.

The village was little more than thirty or forty mud-packed, thatch-roofed huts strung in a loose community and located in a wide clearing between the forest and a river (fed by the stream at which we had encountered the Berserkers four miles north). An independent, non-political tribe, they were dedicated to surviving on Thear with the most comfort and the least interference possible, but would fight viciously any intrusion on their society. And intrusions did occur.

Thear was an ideal setting for experimental government, and some of the surrounding tribes illustrated the wide range of existing settlements. Within a forty mile radius of that point on the continent, there was a communistic village so well refined that all of its inhabitants were starving at the same rate, a democratic setup where a man couldn't defend his home or mate from outside attack without calling a towncouncil meeting, and a pair of communities separated by only twenty miles, yet utilizing radically diverse philosophies. The first was male dominated and kept all females as slaves, and the second was run by women who treated men as creatures less than human. There were several settlements where fruit and vegetable gathering was performed only once or twice weekly (regretfully at that) and the remaining days were spent in strung-out ecstasy chewing on hallucinatory herbs. But the most common tribes on Thear couldn't actually be referred to as such, because they consisted of now wild Earth children who had been abandoned on the planet during their earliest years and roamed the forests and jungles in widely-feared packs. Sure, you could set up any imaginable form of government on Thear, and all you had to do was defend it against starvation, dissolution, assimilation, and common destruction by marauders.

"Looks like you have everything in this place but those make-believe commune farms we heard about back on Earth," I commented.

"Oh, we have those, also," Doc corrected me.

"Yeah? Where?"

"About two thousand miles east of here on the other coastline. They are the original colonies set up in '02 for the first settlers, and a select number of lucky exiles are yet unloaded there on every shipload. All of the TV specials took place there as well as the personal investigation undertaken by concerned political figures. They discourage immigrants from 'the bush,' by the way."

Doc showed Holly and myself the primitive, but effective solid waste dump the village used, the feeder stream for drinking water (which they accepted on faith as unpolluted from further upstream), and the cave that we were to room in while deciding on whether to stay or move on. But finally, almost reluctantly, we came to a tiny, particularly pitiful-looking hut.

"This belongs to Vega," Starett said, "and she has been wanting to see you since you arrived."

"And who's Vega?" I asked while sampling a well-done leg of the local equivalent of a pig.

"You could call her the village matriarch, though she wields no practical influence. Chronologically, she's only twenty-six or so, but she's lived here longer than any of us." He paused thoughtfully. "She was abandoned at about the age of three and managed somehow to survive on her own in this area. Naturally, she's rather... unstable mentally, but protocol dictates that all new arrivals be presented before her for inspection and renaming."

"Renaming?" asked Holly.

Doc grinned self-consciously. "Yes, her demi-mystical sense of logic says that magical names can be given to all people to protect their spirits from devils and associated evil influences. My own title was 'the Owl,' no doubt referring to my pedantic speech patterns."

"Wow, this is going to be loads of fun," I muttered as I licked the juice from my fingers.

The hut was indeed small, especially when the three of us

crowded into its gloomy interior for our audience with the Old Woman of Thear. And, twenty-six or not, she certainly looked old. It was easy to look at the skinny, angular frame squatting on the mud floor by the opposite wall and tell how hard the first lonesome years had been on her. Weather and privation had lined her face quickly and tightened her arms and legs to lanky extensions of her slender body. Her hair was long, black, and stringy, some of her teeth were missing, and she had a nervous tick at the left corner of her mouth. But the eyes were clear and glinting, revealing a life that still ran swiftly in her veins. In addition to a divided nose, she had webbed fingers and toes.

"Greetings, our Vega," said Doc as he stooped to a level with her alive eyes. "We have two new visitors."

She looked critically at us. "New, new," she agreed in a high voice. "Dey are new to dis place. Dey hav been here two week, no more. Is Vega right?"

"Less than two," I nodded. "Not one, yet."

She cackled and nodded back to me. "I know, Vega know. Za groun' es my frien' an' tell me much. Name?"

"Pardon?" asked Holly.

"Name, bitchey, tell Vega you name!"

"I'm Holly Gylbre, and this is Eli Harper. We're from Earth," she replied, speaking excessively loudly.

"No, no, no, no." Vega shook her head hard. "No name like dat. Walk aroun'."

We looked to Doc, who shrugged in a helpless fashion. Humor her, he seemed to say, she's the founding mother. So we walked to and fro in the limited area available, our uneasiness poring out like acrid smog. Soon enough, she raised her hand and allowed us to stop.

"You gotta hav new name on you, dead sure. No one know Vega name. Dey cal me name of star in za sky, but Vega name only Vega know, so to live long and full."

I turned to Holly, remembering a similar, though more articulate conversation we'd had aboard the shuttle.

"You girl, little bitch, you be careful or you die quick, cause you unfit for here. I call you . . . Caribou, dumb an' scaredy. An' you, stupid—"

"Me?" I answered.

"Yes, bastid. You show no respec', za groun' say you not bravest on Thear, sure, but Vega like za way you move, quiet. You strong?"

"Some."

"Zen Vega call you Cat, like animal of jungle. Right?"

"Right, right," I agreed, looking longingly at the doorway.

"So you use it, right?"

"Always."

"An' you, Caribou, you don tell nobody true name, right?"

Holly was actually intimidated. "Well, yes, ma'am, if you say so."

"Vega say. Now, go."

"Thanks for a really entertaining—" I began.

"Get out! Vega tired now, asses!"

We got out, believe me.

Finnegan was the toughest, most free-spirited, and least dependable womanizer in that particular section of Thear. He lived in the village only because he could endure none of the more organized governments offered on the rest of the continent. He had a forceful personality, especially with the female of the species, a casual outspokenness, and absolutely no sense of loyalty or respect. For a strange reason, he was rapidly gaining an unhealthy disrespect for me, as well.

The tall Irishman met us coming out of Vega's hut and grinned as we blinked in the brilliant Capella sunlight. "Been in to see mamaloi, have you?" he commented.

"Yeah; I feel like I've just been christened and somebody should sign the birth certificate. That is one weird woman," I said.

"Maybe, but she *has* had a difficult life under extreme conditions," pointed out Doc.

"She's crazy," Finnegan stated simply. "And she gives people crazy names. What's yours, baby?"

Holly looked up. "Me? Um, I think she said Caribou, or something like that."

"'Caribou,' 'reindeer, it fits. But that bag never saw any reindeer. Sounds like something the Brain would have told her."

Starett nodded. "We did speak once about—"

"What about you, slugger?" Finnegan casually interrupted the other.

"More common, I'm afraid. She liked the way I walked, so she bestowed Cat upon me. Didn't think much of my intelligence, though." I added.

"Hmm, maybe she's right. You know, she called me Jackal, can you believe that? Jackal! Like the old bat had the right to assign personalities. She's out of her skull."

52

Starett was evidently becoming nervous at Finnegan's emotional buildup, and he coughed suggestively in our direction. I picked up the cue with, "Hey, Doc, weren't you going to show us those 'coconut bombs' you were talking about this morning?"

"That's right, I was, wasn't I? We'll have to walk over to the pit on the southside."

"So let's go. I'm getting hungry, and I want to be able to distinguish between coconut bombs and the real thing before I go foraging for myself," I said, beginning to walk.

"Now, don't you two forget your 'spirit names,' hear? Old Vega might just cast a spell over you if you do." Finnegan's tone was condescendingly mocking.

"Don't worry, Jackal old boy, I always wanted a nickname, even if it has to be plain and everyday. See you later."

He smiled, but coldly. "Yes, yes you will."

My brain was slow that day; I was far away from the lean, but muscular Finnegan before the real significance of the dog-cat allegory hit me.

We met most of the rest of the villagers that day and found them to be much like Chuck Garner and Sheila Roen, friendly, open, but with their welcome never fully concealing their fierce independence. They—we—had all been rejected by a structured society and expelled from the planet of our births. I understood why almost everyone in that area was determined to guard themselves against any other governments that could remove any of the rights left to them.

Actually, not all of the villagers were like that. One in particular could not have cared less about the workings of government or the affairs of more influential minds. Like Vega, no one knew his real name, or if he had one, but everyone called him by his "given" name of Thumper.

To me, "Thumper" conjured up memories of cartoon animals capering charmingly across a World Library film screen. But, though he did resemble an animalistic caricature of a human being, Thumper was no cartoon. He had wandered out of the jungle one day and decided to stay.

A little under four feet tall, Thumper weighed close to two hundred pounds, much of it spread across his massive shoulders and chest. His knotted arms hung ape-like to just below his knees, and the simian appearance was furthered by his large, prognathous head and long, frizzled hair. The most oddly out of place part of his physique was his undercarriage, consisting of tiny white legs that looked totally incapable of supporting his heavy upper portion. He talked very infrequently, using one or two words only when he did, never interferred with others or invited interference, and possessed the explosive power and savagery to handle any ten Berserkers at once.

Quiet, a terrific hunter, apparently little more intelligent than the ape he resembled, Thumper was the equivalent of the village idiot. But he was a respected and usually well-liked idiot.

That was our new home. Carved out of the wilderness, with that same wilderness surrounding it, we found the loose assocation of individuals to be an easy group to exist with and fight for when the occasion arose. Chuck Garner was reluctantly the closest thing to a leader that they had, and the problems of personal survival were reduced to the basic concepts of finding one's food and catching it.

But the life—basic, dangerous, and open—was missing something, something quite vital. And I wouldn't realize just what it was until an extraordinary set of circumstances evolved six months later.

4

"Shana Wilbanks"

"Do pass me the potation, old boy," I said to Jeffrey Nichols in a casually bored tone while a warm afternoon breeze drifted past my half open eyes.

"My pleasure, Colonel," he replied. As he passed the tall, half-filled gourd, I had to search for it among the dark hues of the tree we were both reclining in, because Jeff had completely let himself go since arriving on Thear and unconsciously blended in with the immediate background.

My grasping hand closed around the natural jug, and I guided another swallow of the mildly fermented fruit juices into my mouth. It stung, brought tears to my eyes, but the spreading warmth that hit my stomach still elicited a thankful sigh from me. "Just exquisite, that's all. What's on today's agenda?"

"Supper. My cupboard is bare, and I'm afraid that stalking meals is not the most impressive of my long list of talents."

"You? The greatest natural camouflage expert in the hemisphere?"

"The same. I can go invisible to the eye, but what am I supposed to do about my smell?"

"Bathe."

I was savoring the juice of my verbal triumph when a brief metallic flash of light zipped through the clear sky over our heads and startled the entire village. Though I'd never seen one from the ground while on Thear, I knew almost instinctively what the flash was.

"What in the hell was *that*?" Jeff demanded.

"Shuttle," I said, hanging off the limb, "coming down."

I dropped to the ground amid the welter of locals and immediately had my guess confirmed by others who'd seen the phenomenon before. We all agreed that it was a shuttle craft and that it was landing (or crashing) just to the east of us. What we didn't agree on was the reason behind its arrival.

"More freaks, that's obvious enough," Jeff said loudly.

"Maybe not," disagreed Gary "Skunk" Eisel. "You were on the last shipment; how long ago was that?"

"About six months," replied Jeff.

"Six months and twelve days," corrected Doc Starett.

"Okay, six months. Since it takes seven months one way for the low drive shipment, they never make two trips within such a short space of time. Haven't had two transfer convoys in tandem for the last five, six years."

"It does imply that this is a special shipment," agreed Doc.

"So why don't we find out?" asked Sheila Roen, who had just walked seductively up.

"I think she's got something there," Jeff said to me. I leered for the occasion.

Stepping carefully through the squeaking assembly of confused elves, eleven of us, including Finnegan, Chuck, and Thumper, made our way quickly into the forest in the direction that the shuttle seemed to have grounded. As quick as we were, Horace the Monkey was quicker. Because of my strength and agility, I was pretty good in the trees, but the Monkey, who was built like a three foot tall one, outstripped me in all arboreal categories. He moved expertly through the high, twining branches, and could double that speed in the thicker jungle areas. I elected to stay on the ground with my companions.

We moved swiftly enough, and covered a mile and a half before Horace met us on his excited way back, screaming at the top of his chalk-scratch voice, "It's down, boys, it's down!"

"Anybody come out?" Chuck called up to him.

"Not yet, no, not yet, but it didn't crash, so they will!" He turned and dashed toward the ship. We speeded up.

It was a shuttle craft from one of the transfer ships, we saw as we peered from the concealment of the bush. It didn't seem to be in any distress, but it just sat there like an unopened gift. A Trojan Horse, maybe.

"I don't like it," Eisel said nervously. "They don't just set down an expensive piece of equipment like that for no reason."

He was shushed by Chuck as something began happening to the

56

ship. Its doors spread open, and the ramp extended carefully down to the thick grass beneath it. For a moment, it was quiet again before the figures walked out. They were W. H. O. flunkies, as we could tell from the uniforms and drawn stunners, but the bulky, graying man and the slim, black-haired girl who followed were dressed in civilian clothes and carried themselves with the pride and assurance of wealth and genetic purity.

"Well, lookit that," whispered Finnegan gleefully, "we got some 'normals' with us. Slumming, I guess."

"That's World Congressman Farrell Wilbanks; I recognize him from a news release," Doc informed us. "The release came out three years ago, but, allowing for the proper maturation, I would say that the girl is his daughter Shana."

"What are they doing here?" Sheila asked.

"Political exiles," I ventured.

"Nah," said Chuck. "Not Kurtz' style. His opponents all have 'accidents.'"

Behind the civilians came three more W. H. O. men, each carrying projectile guns and long, wooden clubs, both out of date weapons that were seldom seen on Earth. I noticed Horace high in a tree and hoped that he could control his chattering a little longer.

The civilian man spoke, and I strained to catch the words, "So, Lei Tow, there are no more Farms or developed areas on this planet, eh?"

"No, sir," the head W. H. O. man answered. "The ones surrounding the space port are all we have."

The girl looked startled.

"That is contrary to all of the official press notices that the World Health Organization feeds us. Do you just abandon the poor fools in rough territory, like this to scratch out a living or die?"

"Yes, sir, that is standard procedure."

"Why not shoot them and have done with it? Seems much more humane."

"Director Kurtz doesn't wish to destroy the mutants, but neither does he want them to construct a form of civilization that may, someday, rival that of natural human beings. It is policy to carry out regular surveillance throughout the planet and destroy settlements that seem too advanced. Other than the controlled Farms, of course."

"Of course. You realize, I hope, that I shall have to include all of this in my official report?"

"I realize, sir."

The girl was staring frightenedly at the surrounding bush and the club wielding crewmen. She stared directly at us, but didn't see us.

Congressman Wilbanks continued, "I find this entire setup morally reprehensible. I have long suspected that Kurtz handled this mutant affair in an irrational and illegal fashion, but I've had no proof until now. Kurtz may be the most powerful individual on Earth, but my report to the remaining sane members of the governing classes might upset the applecart enough to straighten out this degraded situation."

"Daddy," whispered the girl, "let's go. I'm *scared*."

"Sir," the W. H. O. representative continued, "Director Kurtz is only insuring the welfare of the true human race and allowing these savages as much of a pleasurable life as their deformities would permit, anyway."

"Nonsense, man. These people could never threaten us." Wilbanks took his daughter's arm and turned toward the ship. "I've seen quite enough of this place; let's go."

The three men with clubs stepped in front of them, blocking the ramp. "I'm afraid that won't be necessary, sir."

"What is this?" Wilbanks roared, his face suddenly crimson.

"Orders, sir, just orders. Director Kurtz realized the danger you posed to the rational community of Earth and provisions for your removal were arranged." The man raised his club.

Wilbanks instantly knew the truth. Shoving his daughter roughly away, he shouted for her to run before a hard chop to the back of his neck drove him to his knees. The five men were on them like a pack of hungry wolves.

At first, we were confused, not knowing whether to attack the armed men or keep our noses safe, but, while seeing the sadists happily torture the bleeding, crying girl as she crawled at their feet, the strain was too much for Finnegan. "Bastards!" he screamed as he leaped from the brush. We all followed.

The W. H. O. men never had a chance. We covered them before they realized what had happened, clawing and rending in our hate and rage. Thumper picked the largest man up above his head and twisted his trunk in opposite directions while Finnegan smashed another's head like so much jelly. All five were dead or dying within seconds.

They had left the pilot on board, as we found out when the doors began to close for emergency liftoff, but Thumper squeezed through a small rift just before they clamped shut and was quickly inside. We followed his progress by the sounds of crashing metal and erratic gunfire until a prolonged cry of anguish told us that he had located the trapped man and the battle was over. His shaggy head reappeared momentarily through the still open doors.

"Doc!" shouted Chuck. "Into the tub; see if we can use any of its systems!"

With no word of assent, Starett scrambled up into the ship to replace Thumper, who left it. We checked the bodies, finding all five of the exposed W. H. O. men dead from assorted hand-inflicted wounds. Looking over the still form of Congressman Wilbanks, I found that our aid had arrived seconds too late, and he had been killed by a half-crushed skull, not to mention various other breaks and tears, but I felt no real emotion either way upon viewing my first up-close dead body. Wilbanks had sounded sympathetic to our plight, but his speech had been filled with the usual misconceptions and prejudices applied to mutants.

"Hey, the girl's alive!" Jeff yelled.

We assembled closely about her and saw the shallow breaths and one throbbing vein in her neck. She was badly beaten about the face and body, as her torn clothing showed, but no single critical wound could be found.

"We need Joanna," Chuck muttered as he wiped some of the blood from her eyes. "She knows more about medicine than any of us."

"Let Doc take a look at her," Eisel suggested. "He knows something about everything."

"After he looks the ship over," Chuck told him.

Thumper ambled over to the group and looked down on the girl with a minimum of interest. Chuck squatted before the ape-like man and stared into his face, trying to monopolize his scattergun attention. "Thumper," he said clearly, "the man in the ship, what happened to the man?"

Thumper gave him an expression that said, "What else?" "Kill 'im," he answered in a rumbling grunt like a bass drum.

"Did he call for help? On the radio?"

"No. Ripped it out. Broke 'is neck."

"Good work, good work. He didn't give the port his position," Chuck sighed.

Finnegan spoke up, "Why th' hell did they kill 'em this way? Why not just put a bullet in their heads?"

"They needed their bodies," Jeff replied with easy comprehension. "They needed them beaten to death so they could take them back to Earth and claim we did it."

"That sounds good," Chuck said. Then to Thumper, "You're sure the pilot didn't radio back any message?"

The other merely stared at him through half-lidded eyes.

Doc stuck his head out the partially open doors and signalled to us.

"Anything in there of use?" called out Garner.

"Nothing, really. The controls have been ripped and smashed by Thumper and are full of bullet holes. The power cells have been torn loose and are draining at this moment. Naturally, we can use the metal and synthetic fiber as raw materials, but this ship will never lift again without a major repair job at an equipped center." As an afterthought, he added, "The pilot's dead."

"Suicide rate is horrible these days," Jeff assured us.

I nodded sympathetically.

"Come on out, then," Chuck said. "See if it's okay to carry the girl back to camp. She might pull through."

Starett did so, informing us of no more serious obvious injury than a concussion and broken fingers on her left hand. So, using some cane poles as a makeshift stretcher, we hauled her back over the forest trail to Joanna's hut, not sure if our trouble would pay off.

As we left the landing site, I walked over to Jeff, who was standing and gazing at a mangled body. "Worst case of natural causes I've ever seen," I said.

It was his turn to solemnly nod.

I awoke to crying and screaming from next door. That would be Joanna's hut, only fifty feet away, but the feminine voice certainly didn't sound like the wise-cracking nurse-doctor of our settlement. In fact, it was a rather new voice to my ears: Shana Wilbanks'.

"No, no, no!" she was screaming over and again. "He's *not* dead, not Daddy, too!"

I could faintly hear Joanna making soothing, hushing sounds, but they failed in their intentions miserably.

"Oh! I hurt . . . all over," the girl sobbed. "Why did they do it?"

"Here," said Joanna, "put this on your face. It'll make—"

"Don't *touch* me! Don't touch me, you-you monster!"

Jeeze, I thought, rolling out of the sack with a grinding and popping orchestration. My stomach had its feelings hurt because I had been neglecting it, and I hate to be at odds with any part of my anatomy. So I snatched up a half-inedible pear-shaped vegetable and began to munch. Holly was nowhere around, but since she was usually out at the river washing her few articles of clothing in the mornings, I looked no further than the doorway. Having achieved the considerable feat of walking that far, I slumped in the shade before opening the crude door and watching the world unfold as I ate.

It wasn't long before I wasn't alone. Chuck stumbled through the door blinking in the sudden gloom as opposed to the brilliant sunlight. "And a good morning, Cat," he greeted me.

Cat. The nickname had stuck after Vega bestowed it on me, Jeff's reason being that Eli sounded too "holy," too Old Testament for common usage, and now only Holly called me by my proper name with any regularity.

"And a redundancy to you," I said. "Have a seat and some breakfast. Or either."

"No, thanks, I've eaten, and there are too many things to do to sit down."

"Like for instance?"

"Like for instance getting off this shithole of a planet," he answered.

I continued to peel a cakefruit with what I hoped was obvious calm. "Nice project. How do you propose to pull it off?"

"Using three main components: diversion, aptitude, and political power."

"Now, why didn't I think of that?"

"Number one, diversion. The main force of the Earth port over on the coast will very soon be marshalled to look for that Wilbanks girl."

"Think so?"

"I know so. Right now, the head joes don't know if Shana or her father are safely dead, since their ship didn't report back, and, after this tremendous political gamble they have taken by trying to murder them, they have to be sure that the plans have been completed. Last night, a lighted shuttle passed over us twice looking for wreckage.

"Pretty soon they'll have every available ship combing this entire area, leaving only a token force manning the port. Meanwhile, we will be escorting Miss Wilbanks *to* the port, not running from it. That's the diversion."

"But we're still on this scenic funspot," I pointed out.

"Number two is aptitude or ability. Bull Mumbali spent a year and a half at a Farm less than a mile from the port, and he was in the place so much on deliveries that he knows it like the hair on his stomach. He'll get us by the remaining troops and into a hot ship that—"

"Aha, and how are we supposed to get a shuttle into a mother ship and get *that* monster out of orbit?"

"We don't. We don't even hijack a shuttle. Earth has a small fleet of contact ships that carry government reports and instructions between the planets on a regular basis, something around every three months, sort of like a space age Pony Express. These little boats don't carry nearly the payload of the big ships and can make the crossing in less than half the time and still retain a margin of supralight drive safety."

"And I suppose these things fly themselves?"

"Practically. The navigation is handled by the on-board computers, but a human pilot is required for the overall flight. That's where Doc Starett comes in; he'll handle the ship on the trip itself and get us through Earth's early warning system into a safe, unobserved landing."

"Let's see, that only leaves political power."

"And political power is the daughter of Congressman Farrell Wilbanks. We get her down, smuggle her to see some other influential bigwigs—easily recommended, I'm sure, by Shana herself— she explains the real situation and the murder plans Kurtz instituted, and, bingo, total revision of the system, the downfall of James William Kurtz, and back home for the prodigals."

"Do I fit in some way?"

"Damn right you do. The way I see it, just to get from here across a couple of thousand miles of jungle to the space port, we're going to need a solid force of fighting men. No fewer than twelve, no more than twenty."

"Why so many just to get through the jungle?"

He shook his head. "I thought you'd learned, Cat. For every non-hostile tribe we meet out there, we'll have to fight, or outrun, three unfriendly ones. And there are animals out there, lord, bigger than anything walking on Earth. Dinosaurs. On a trip like this, I'd rather have you than any six others on this planet."

"I'll find you seven volunteers."

He ignored that. "The ones I've chosen already are Bull, Shana, and myself, of course, Finnegan, Thumper, Hadji, and you, if you accept."

"Sounds like you've got enough to fight off half the continent if I don't. Hadji and Bull could tear down a granite mountain if it suited their needs. Thumper would stand a good chance against both of them at once. Finnegan... well, you can't deny his ability, but can you really trust him? He's not the most self-sacrificing guy I've met on Thear."

"He's an unreliable bastard, all right, but who could replace him?"

"What about Jeff?"

"Good selection, but he's no Finnegan."

"Hmm. What about guides, scouts?"

"There aren't any real guides, as such, but Horace would be perfect in the roll of scout, as at home in the trees as he is. Counting you and Nichols, that makes nine. We've got plenty of beef, but we'll need backups to fill in for those who won't make it."

"Another inviting facet you can list on the promotional ads," I grunted. "But, I guess you inspire loyalty to have these people ready to chance it all with you."

He looked away. "Well, they're not actually ready, yet. You're the first guy I've sounded the idea on."

"What? You haven't convinced Bull or Doc or Finnegan... or even Shana?"

"Only because I haven't talked to them. I'm sure they'll be glad to give anything a try just to get out of here."

The recruiting of talent turned out to be an all-day job and, despite a mid-afternoon snack of fruit and vegetables, I was gnawingly hungry as Capella slid down the darkening sky and the night sounds began. We had selected twenty prospective members for our journey, and thirteen had accepted, the rest being Hadji, Horace, Jeff, Michael "Bear" Bolger, Ellen Polanska, Gary "Skunk" Eisel, Lewis Chang, and Chuck and myself. Everyone chosen could travel light, hard, and long, and they would provide a degree of protection that would undoubtedly be needed until we succeeded or (as I was yet half-convinced) were stopped. One valuable selection who had refused was Joanna March, who had informed us that she had not planned to get her tail shot off on some hare-brained scheme that had about as much chance of success as a proverbial sphere of frozen water in the place where angels don't go.

We both tried to change her mind, but were met with a solid wall of refusal.

"Let's call it a day, Chuck," I suggested as I watched the stars come out.

I bade him a good night and faded into the forest for a kill. I wanted to make the strike as simple and swift as possible because, though we lived in a relatively safe area of the planet, there were a certain number of animals out in the night that might view me as a tasty treat for the kiddies back at the nest. I was in luck; I killed a pig and carried it back to my hut within an hour.

Holly was there, tending a small fire and nibbling on some greens. She looked up a bit petulantly as I dumped the bleeding body at her feet.

"Just get it brown, will you? I'm starving," I told her, falling to the floor.

As Holly worked, she talked, mostly about inconsequential matters, but finally bringing up my activities of the day. "I heard you and Chuck were 'interviewing' several different people around the village today. What was that all about?"

As quickly as I could, I related the story to her and named those we had chosen to go on the expedition.

"You might really get back to Earth? Oh, Eli, can I go, too?" she asked excitedly.

Holly Gylbre was, as Vega had pointed out, unfit for survival on Thear, both physically and mentally. She had never actually adjusted to the floral existence that she had been thrust into; therefore, as a member of the force that would try for all of the marbles, I could see her only as a liability.

"Aw, you'd be safer in some other village. We probably won't make it, anyway," I said.

"But I'd rather die in that than spend the rest of my life here with no hope!" she answered. "It's not the people—they're all in the same situation— but it's the way we've been treated. We're human, too!"

"But, hell, Holly, I know it's easy to talk about dying 'gloriously' right now, in a hut roasting a pig, but when that arrow slips between your ribs or a bunch of slobbering halfwits catch you, it's a different story. Find somebody that you can stay with and, if we make it all the way, the lid'll blow off. Maybe you'll find yourself back home without taking the first risk."

Her voice was quiet, but sincere. "I want to go with you, Eli."

I sighed, "Damn. Okay, I'll ask Chuck about it tomorrow."

We ate in silence, and I took that cool, soothing dip in the calmly flowing river, sat in the breeze at the top of a tree for a time, and was back in my hut by Thear's midnight. Holly lay motionless on the straw mat, her glistening skin lit only by the dying embers of the fire. I didn't bother to rekindle it. Instead, I slid down to my place beside her and slipped my right arm around her smooth, cold waist and drew her to me. Later, we both slept.

5

"The Challenger Mutants"

My awakening was, to say the least, rude.

Though the hut was still cloaked in darkness of a comfortable night, a sudden uproar from the center of the village shocked my sensitive ears to life with painful abruptness. I rolled to my haunches between Holly and the door as a loud shuffling beyond it announced an imminent visitation.

"Eli?" Holly whispered sleepily.

"Hush!" I tensed for a leap.

The door pulled open and a tall, dark shape blotted out the little moonlight from Thear's twin satellites. "Cat! Cat! Unplug and get out here! We're under attack!"

It was Chuck, made taller by my expectant imagination, and I restrained myself just before leaping at him. "What's going on?"

"I don't know! Horace is hysterical, and there seems to be some sort of firefight just east! I think it's the troops from spaceport!"

I snatched up my shorts and walked my legs into them as I went for the door. Outside, the entire clearing was a madhouse as mutants of all physical variations ran about waving torches at imagined attackers, and the tens of newly arrived elves spilled out of their cave in high-pitched confusion. A dull red glow pulsed from somewhere over in the forest to my left.

"Good lord!" declared a familiar voice next to my ear.

I glanced about, knowing that he would be an undetectable night black. "Materialize, willya? I don't need to hold a conversation with a ghost right now!"

Jeff's pale face appeared from the air wearing a smile. "How's this?" he asked.

"It'd be better if you weren't so ugly. What's going on?"

"Hell if I know. Looks like a freak riot to me. Whatdaya mean 'ugly'?"

I caught sight of Chuck and two others clustered about the small body of Horace, the sentry, and very excited over what he seemed to be saying. Holly emerged from the hut wrapped in an antelope skin, and the three of us plowed through the buzzing crowd to where Garner stood.

"I was asleep, I was asleep!" Horace was shouting.

"You told us," Chuck said to him. "Now calm down, take it easy. What happened?"

"They came down in the ship like before and woke me up! They landed there a'side the other one! I said-I said, 'They found the ship!'"

"How many were there?" Finnegan asked with a sneer at the little man.

"One ship, only one!"

"No, stupid, how many people?"

"A lot! Thirty, forty with guns and flame throwers! They dug up the bodies, all of 'em, and said, 'Where's the girl? Where's the girl?'"

"Get Shana out here," Chuck ordered to Doc Starett. "We can't afford to lose her now. Then what, Horace?"

"The Berserkers! I said, 'You'd better get Chuck right here, Horace! You'd better get him quick!' The Berserkers attacked from the woods, but the men shot them with bullets and fire! They set the forest on fire!"

"It's a damn sure bet that they'll head this way," said Chuck darkly. "They've got to find the girl and kill her. God, they'll burn this place to the ground!"

"We'd better get our tails moving," Finnegan said. "If we set up in the trees just outside the clearing, we can surprise 'em from above—"

"Are you crazy?" Jeff asked. "The kid just told us that they wiped out a whole tribe of Berserkers! They're not playing with pop guns, you know!"

Finnegan angrily narrowed his eyes and said nothing.

"He's right," Chuck agreed. "We wouldn't stand a chance against their armament. We've got to run now and evacuate the whole village."

"Let's go," I said.

"Wait a minute. Let's get the rest of our group up, because, like it or not, we're going to start our trip a day early. There's so much I needed to do—"

A sudden burst of automatic gunfire from the forest galvanized us into action. Wading through the mass of people, we rounded up the pre-selected group of mutants to accompany us and spread the evacuation word among the rest. In a surprisingly short span of time, we all stood before Chuck's hut, with our number swelled to fifteen by the addition of Holly and Sheila Roen.

Finnegan had arrived by stamping heedlessly through the fleeing elves, and he casually kicked one little woman out of his way.

"You stupid animal!" she squealed at him.

With a mean smile, Finnegan raised his foot over her ten inch body again.

"Hold it!" I shouted, grabbing his arm and pulling him off.

He whirled on me with a curse and a wild growl. "I'll kill you, you sonofabitch!"

"Not now; it'll get us both burned by those maniacs out there," I pointed out, indicating the noisily approaching troops.

"I'll get you later," he promised me with a deep hiss.

Holly stooped to the fallen girl. "Are you all right?" she asked.

"I think the clumsy lummox broke my leg!" she answered, grasping the tiny extremity in obvious pain. She looked over her shoulder at the rest of her people, who were swiftly disappearing in the underbrush. "Hey! Wait! Wait for me!" she cried shrilly.

They either didn't hear or refused to stop.

"Please, come back!" Her eyes glowed wetly in the torchlight.

"Eli?" Holly looked at me. "We can't leave her here alone."

I nodded.

She picked the doll-like girl up in her hands and began talking to her.

"Everybody here?" Chuck called over the dying din.

"Too many!" Finnegan called back. "Nobody told me that this little bitch had been selected." He pointed to Holly, whom he had openly disliked and continually baited since she had refused his advances after we arrived.

"Caribou?" asked Chuck.

"She wants to go with us," I answered.

"Okay by me, but she's your responsibility, Cat," he said.

"Great," I muttered to myself.

We moved out of the nearly deserted village then, taking up a formation that assured the safety of our most important members.

Garner, Finnegan, Thumper, and I led the way; Hadji, Jeff, Bear Bolger, Ellen Polanska, and Lew Chang protected our stern; Bull, Shana, and Doc were safely cloistered in the middle and flanked by Gary Eisel, Sheila, and Holly and her doll girl. Horace, who could never stay on the ground for too long, scouted through the trees a few yards ahead of us. Once out of range of the port troops, Chang, Thumper, Ellen, and I planned to take turns helping him keep watch for massed enemies or possible traps to avoid.

To detour the burning forest and Kurtz's men, we hit it out on a northern march by following the river upstream from the concealment inside the tree line. This would take us quite a few miles off our original course, but, by allowing a gradual eastern curve, it would have us well away from the search area by daylight.

The long march had begun.

Whether by virtue of our planning or by dumb luck, we didn't come in contact with a single trooper on that first night's walk. Our closest brush came when a humming shuttle craft rose above the tree tops just a mile to the south of us. But, despite our fears, it continued on a western passage and disappeared into the remaining night.

After three hours of steady tramping through the high-topped forest, we were on a level eastern course along which we could see the rose highlights of the rising sun. There were plenty of voices raised in favor of stopping for breakfast and rest, but Chuck kept us going, reasoning that we would need all of the miles we could get between us and our former dwelling place.

Holly drifted up to my side and held the elf girl she had carried since our departure. "She doesn't want to come with us," Holly said.

I looked at the slight, but noticeable swelling in the girl's leg. "Doesn't look to me like she's got much choice," I replied.

"You don't have to shout, you big ape," she squeaked back to me. "Would you please tell this featherbrained broad to put me down so I can try to pick up the trail of my people before it disappears?"

"Is her leg busted?" I asked Holly.

"I don't think so, but I'm sure she can't walk on it."

"Left here, you'd make a bite-sized burger for the first carnivorous animal that came along," I noted. "So, like I said, you're along for the ride."

"Oh, great," she sighed. "Meanwhile my people are going top

speed in the opposite direction. Why should I get all of the Good Samaritans?"

"You might get to go back to Earth," Holly told her.

"And that's good? Are you brutes so dumb that you can't see that I don't *want* to go back there?"

I didn't know what to say, so I said nothing. She kept staring up at us, awaiting a reply. Eventually, I admitted, "I can see your side, but if we let you go, it would be murder, nothing else. We're responsible for your separation from your tribe and the injury to your leg, so, naturally, we want to help. But I'm willing to set you loose here, if that's really what you want."

"Well, what can I say? I don't want to go it alone and half-crippled like this, and I'm sure you won't turn back long enough to find my own people."

"We'd be seen by the troops," I said quietly.

"So, okay, I suppose. For now."

The sun had struggled up forty-five degrees on its long haul across the sky before Chuck finally called a halt for breakfast. He probably wouldn't have stopped that soon, but we had stumbled onto a large pool of fresh water and a veritable grove of fruit trees; the opportunity was too good to miss.

Shana Wilbanks had been conspicuously silent throughout our march and, like Jeff and Holly, I couldn't resist the temptation to drop next to her and see how her attitude toward "gawfs" had changed. She sat by the pool nibbling cautiously at an olive fruit and looking tired and somewhat frightened. When I sat heavily at her side, she pulled away a couple of feet and eyed me suspiciously. I hadn't thought how savage my upper fur made me look until that moment, and I felt a mixture of anger and embarrassment.

"How's the hand?" I asked to break the ice.

"It hurts," she answered, resting the crudely splinted and bandaged member in her lap. "Why?"

"Why not? It beats talking about anthrax."

To my relief, Jeff collapsed next to her opposite side and immediately faded into the background, except for his eyes and teeth. "This a private club or can any old gawf sit in?" he asked.

"You keep your dues up, and you can even use the executive washroom," I said. "It's that big bush over there."

"How are you feeling?" asked Holly, who had also joined us (minus the elf girl). Unlike my own, her concern was sincere.

But Shana was little more open with her. "I think I'll live, if it matters to you people."

"Darn right it matters to us," Jeff told her. "You're our ticket out of this dump."

Her smooth face was nervously drawn, and she had pulled her long dark hair to the back of her head, though she had nothing to tie it there. She was dirty and her once elegant travelling suit was torn and blood-stained, but she still retained a measure of superiority in her voice when she said, "Suppose I don't go along with your hopeless little scheme?"

"Why, I never considered that. I guess we'd just have to leave you somewhere out there," he indicated the deepening forest, "alone. After all, trapped here, you'd soon become one of us."

This possibility didn't seem to please her at all. She actually sniffed aristocratically.

"What you need, baby, is for someone to put a tan on that prim little butt of yours." Finnegan had arrived practically unnoticed, and his voice fairly dripped with venom.

"Hey, lay off, Finnegan," Jeff said.

"Shut up. I don't like ingratitude." He squatted among us.

"Ingratitude?" Shana demanded with a little life in her words.

"That's right, you high-classed whore. Who do you think saved your life after those 'loyal soldiers' of Earth beat your old man's brains to jelly? And you talk about not helping us."

Painful memories struck the girl like a physical blow.

"You'll do it, all right, or I'll—"

"Finnegan, please," Holly interrupted him.

He looked at her with a vicious smile. "Later for you, Caribou, like the real deer."

I should have stuffed my mouth full of food and kept it quiet, but my tongue sometimes exhibits dire suicidal tendencies and forges ahead without bothering to consult my brain. This was one of those times. "That's uncommonly coherent language from a bi-ped who, in the past, has had difficulty chewing gum in rhythm." I bit off a chunk of something that tasted vaguely of beef, in a green vegetable, yet.

The lean Irishman stood again and breathed deeply. "Stand up," he said in little more than a whisper.

"Bad for the digestion," I replied.

"I'm going to be bad for your breathing. Get up."

I rose because I knew he would attack me where I sat. "Well, now, we could talk about this."

"You spineless pig!" He lashed out at my head with a right hand, which I ducked while setting myself to land a quick and, hopefully, terminating combination left-right. But I never triggered the punches, as a black form suddenly burst between the two of us.

Both Finnegan and I were at least ten times more powerful than Chuck Garner's normal human muscles, but he had inserted himself in our path with no more hesitation than he would have shown in breaking up a playground quarrel between a pair of six year olds. And, as proof of our respect for his leadership, we stepped back and awaited developments.

"Hold on, you two!" Chuck urged us. "We can't be fighting among ourselves on the *first day*!"

The evening of the fourth day, I drew the second or "split" watch, in which I was to sleep for five hours, watch for five, and sleep away the remainder.

I sat apart from Horace and Lewis Chang, my watch partners, and stared at the fire until it had me practically hypnotized. In this wet, soporific state, that peculiar mental wandering of mine took over, bringing another set of prefabricated memories.

There was one cottage in a tremendous, snow-covered meadow, and one light was on in that cottage. I was tramping slowly toward it, leaving deep, black tracks behind, and I felt warm despite the frosty air and setting sun. It was a sad, yet calm and resigned feeling within my mind.

"Hey, hey," came a voice through the dream. "Aren't you supposed to be guarding me?"

"That's right," I said to Shana Wilbanks, the only person except the three watchers who was still awake. Four days of constant association with sixteen relatively cordial "freaks" had not visibly softened her attitude toward us, and she was still rather haughty and solitary. This was the first time she had ever initiated a conversation with me or, as far as I knew, anyone.

"Do you always sleep on guard duty?"

"Believe it or not, I wasn't asleep, just thinking."

"Do your eyes always glaze over when you 'think'?" she said in a tone that was not so bitingly sarcastic as it once might have been.

Right then, one of the other guards, Lewis Chang, made what appeared to be a casual, friendly stroll over to my side. Half Oriental, he was a short, slender man, but one look told you he was made of steel, guts, and piano wires. Time and again, he had stood over victims who learned too late that appearances can be deceiving. Unlike most of us chosen for the mission, he had no unnatural strength or speed endowments, his own mutation being a back covered in one inch, spike-like bones, but he was a devout student of a group of fighting techniques once known as "the martial arts."

I suspected nothing as he walked over to the tree I was leaning against and squatted below me. "What's up, Lew?" I asked in a not really caring voice.

"We're surrounded," he whispered back through a tight smile.

I opened my mouth, but didn't speak. Holding my head still, my eyes swept the limits of their range looking for intruders in the dense underbrush. I saw no one. "You sure?" I whispered back.

He laughed aloud, as if at some blue joke, and said, "Yep. At least twenty, maybe more. In the trees and on the ground. You didn't hear or smell them because of the rain."

"No chance that they're friendly, I guess?"

"Not much. They have no weapons and don't seem to be wearing any clothing. Probably Throwbacks."

"Start waking," I said, standing. I had always dreaded the day when I would have to face a pack of Throwbacks, not solely because of fear, but also out of some warped sense of justice. They were the original settlers of Thear and, in their own animalistic way, were not responsible as humans. Instinct for survival dictated their moves and allowed them to kill only for food, never for sports or politics. I didn't want to kill any of them, because it would be akin to murdering a retarded brother or sister who had already suffered too much at the hands of "intelligent" humans.

But I didn't want to die, either.

We walked slowly among the sleeping bodies, prodding with our feet at people who sprang instantly into full consciousness. Horace controlled himself enough to follow our lead and not go into a screaming mania. In fact, we had eight people awake before the assault started.

They came at us from the trees and the underbrush, perhaps realing the paralyzing effects of a loud cry coupled with a swift attack, for they screamed like frying souls as they hit us. There were at least thirty, and, though most looked undernourished and stunted, they fought savagely with teeth, nails, and any offensive mutations nature had cast upon them.

Chang and I met the charge first, as the rest scrambled to their feet. Utilizing a shrill, cat-like shriek of his own, Lew became a sudden slashing blur of striking force with four deadly limbs; his legs were as quick and deft as most men's arms, and where he hit, he hurt. I swept up a piece of what would have been firewood and hoped I was fast enough to defuse the crowd about me before any got lucky enough to reach my throat.

God, they just kept coming out of the brush, swarming over us like gigantic bees even before some could make their feet. In a frantic glance, I saw Chuck fall to the ground under a rush that totally covered his body, while Bull Mumbali was tearing them from his own huge body and shaking them unconscious. Flattening one particularly aggressive foe with my fists, I watched as Ellen Polanska—guarding Shana in her pantherish style—was wrestled away from her charge by a pair of the Throwbacks, and I saw our "mealticket" attacked by the engulfing horde.

Holly tried to pull her free, but, lacking any ability, the girl more often called Caribou and Reindeer was quickly forced to the ground. I knew where my duty lay and made my way in that direction. We were basically expendable; Shana was not.

Pulling the screaming animals away from Shana was like picking struggling apples, but, I lifted her now bleeding form to my right shoulder and leaped clear of the melee to the lower branch of a good-sized tree. She clung to the branch hysterically as I dropped back down to fight off four attackers who were already digging their way up the trunk. As I said, I didn't want to hurt or kill them, but they continued to *strike*, never making a move in self-defense, and, caught up in the madness as I was, I went slightly battle-crazy myself.

We seemed to be winning the fight as more and more unconscious Throwbacks fell to the grass, but a few of us were still overmatched or numerically swamped, and I couldn't see Gary Eisel anywhere. I didn't think of it as important at the time. Thumper was emitting drum-roll grunts as he dispatched one attacker after another, and Finnegan was actually laughing as he beat heads in all about him. Doc Starett was giving a surprisingly good account of himself, his four arms allowing him to hold his opponent while he beat him with the others.

Finally, the few remaining raiders retreated, dragging the majority of their wounded and dead behind.

"Show's over," a bleeding Chuck Garner announced as we gathered closer around the waning campfire. "Anybody hurt seriously?"

Everyone was wounded to some degree—I had a gash on my stomach and a companion to it on a thigh— but none seemed worse than Chuck's own cracked rib, which Doc, who had memorized a couple of medical tests and talked extensively with Joanna, was fairly sure he could take care of. Shana was relatively unhurt and still in the tree where I'd left her.

Suddenly Jeff took a mental count and came up short. "Hey, wait a minute. Where's Gary?"

We looked at one another in confusion, but Gary Eisel was not among our number.

"Probably chased one. of the Throwbacks into the brush," Chuck said too quickly and too hopefully. He raised his voice to call, "Gary! Gary Eisel!"

When this drew no response, two or three others began to call, with no more success. In the rain, the sense of smell was dulled considerably, but I noticed Thumper wrinkling his nose repeatedly while the rest of us stood or milled aimlessly about. When the ape man crept silently into the brush, I followed.

We didn't have to go far before discovering the terrible evidence that solved the disappearance. Gary was dead, and his body had been dragged away by the Throwbacks. It had been mutilated.

Coaxing Shana out of the tree proved to be a formidable task, almost as hard as finding dry wood for the fire. But we eventually managed to get her down. Bolger returned soon afterward, and we began the long watch until dawn. At first light, we set out again.

Whatever progress I had made with Shana was totally undone by the unprovoked attack by the Throwbacks. The next day she was once again withdrawn and uncommunicative, hardly speaking to even Sheila and Holly, and eating alone behind hooded, suspicious eyes. This didn't bother me, as long as she did her job once we got back to Earth.

The elf girl (who had told us her name was Linda Simon) spent a good part of her next day's travelling time fashioning a tiny bow and five or six arrows. Against an attack of "giants" like the preceeding night's, the little shafts would be ridiculous weapons, but tipped in her people's special brand of herbal poison, they could prove quite effective.

Our march was subdued, but it ate up the distance. By nightfall, we were thirty to forty miles closer to our destination.

We met tribes as we went and passed through their lands unharmed in the majority of cases, but we occasionally had to fight for our passage. When we came to a large lake during our second week out, we were relieved to have apparently avoided a long detour by securing a transfer on a large wooden barge provided by a local tribe and powered by oars. Halfway across, we were informed by our benefactors that we were to be sold as slaves on the opposite side. The captain had eight crewmen armed with spears, and, for a moment, it looked as if he could back up his prediction.

However, Jeff swiftly blended into virtual transparency and disarmed four of the men before they knew what was happening. Linda jabbed the captain with one of her poisoned arrows, and the sight of their leader going into sudden convulsions and falling overboard, to be swallowed by some dimly seen water beast, persuaded the rest to make our remaining voyage a comfortable one.

Everyone, excluding myself, caught a flu-like disease that caused a delay of two days during our third week, but it left them with no serious aftereffects.

Yes, luck seemed to be with us, and we made surprising time across the wild continent until the start of our second month. That was when we first saw "the Swamp."

6

"The Crossing of Dinosaur Swamp"

"That's called Dinosaur Swamp, and some pretty unhealthy animals prowl around in there."

"How long would this detour take?" Finnegan asked.

"If you go north, a month to get around it. South, maybe two," was his answer.

"Too long. What do you say, Chuck? A month just to cross a strip of land no more than sixty miles wide?"

Bull spoke up, "That's a lot of crap, Chuck. Let's go through it before those murderers pick up our trail. What's a little quicksand?"

Those mental lapses of mine were becoming more frequent and well-defined. They weren't annoying and didn't leave me with the absentmindedness of a sleepwalker, I walked safely and even carried on semi-intelligent conversations while in some, but their increased frequency and clarity did make me a little concerned.

"Cat," interrupted Mike Bolger, who was on watch duty our first night in the swamp, "better quit mooning over what might have been and get some sleep. You're up next, you know."

"Sure, Bear, sure."

Most big, burly fellows on Thear seem to have natural ill dispositions or cultivate them, but Mike, between eight and nine feet tall, was different. Sentenced to Thear because of his huge size and lack of his small fingers and toes, Bolger was an easy-going, intelligent guy who would rather compose his own passable poetry than brawl with friends or enemies. This doesn't mean he *couldn't* brawl when necessary.

He was grinning down at me as I jacked open my ponderous

eyelids, and that did nothing for the good of my temperament. "Gee, I *hate* to wake you," he said with mock sincerity.

"I'll bet," I muttered, propping myself on one elbow. "Your regret is written all over your teeth."

He laughed quietly and opened his mouth to say something else when I saw the sky behind his head suddenly go midnight black. Bolger cried out in surprise and sprawled across me.

Mike weighed somewhere around six hundred muscular pounds, and when he dropped on me like a lead bomb, the air fought its way out of my lungs the way water bursts from a collapsing dam. My own body panicked, and I struggled for freedom while Mike convulsed on top of me. With a sudden surge, I was out from under him, gasping and looking in horror at the thing that had forced him so heavily down upon me.

It was long, maybe four feet, slate gray, and as fat and boneless as some gigantic slug. Four flippers extended from its sides, and, though it had no differentiated head, what seemed to be its anterior was securely fastened to the middle of Mike's back. Its featureless skin seemed drenched in a thick slime and glistened as brightly as Holly's in the moonlight.

"Get it off! Get it off!" Mike was screaming as they thrashed about, he unable to get a hold on the creature.

The others were quickly awakened by the struggle, and we watched in horrified fascination, standing frozen in our places.

"It's a leech of some sort!" Doc shouted. "Tear it off of him! Hurry!"

I was closest and, though Thumper moved fast, I beat down my swelling revulsion and landed on the flabby mound of flesh before he could reach it. The cold ooze squished between my clawing fingers as I sought a firm handhold, but my fists sank into it like dough. Thumper was beside me, ripping in an animal frenzy that he displayed only in battle.

In order to have effective use of its flippers, I realized that the slug would probably have to have a skeletal structure of some kind. While Thumper literally tore the creature apart by fistfuls, I found the hard inner frame and jerked back on it sharply. Mike yelled as the thing was pulled loose from his back, but he added to the effort by swiftly twisting forward. Dark red blood ran from the circular wound when the thing almost pulled free, but it reattached itself as the flipper ripped off in my hands.

I saw what I had to do, and, despite the gut-tearing disgust that boiled up, I did it. Wrapping my arms as far as they would go around its soft body, an action that practically buried my face in a hide that smelled faintly like Earth fish, I stood with the creature, lifted it as high as I was able, and ripped it from Mike's back.

Bolger fell to the ground, choking, and I threw the creature ten feet from myself and began vomiting.

Doc examined Mike's back by the light of a torch, which had burnt down considerably. He had stopped bleeding, and the wound itself, though large, was not very deep.

"I'd like to get something over that for protection against infection," Starett said, "but I haven't seen the correct herbs since we entered this section of land."

"It's okay, Doc," Bolger assured him. "It doesn't hurt anymore."

"The incision isn't dangerously deep," Doc admitted, "but, even though our pre-lift-off injections contained a broad spectrum of local antibodies, the chance of some indigenous organism invading your system is high. Should you recognize any symptoms of illness, let me know."

"Right, first sign," Mike nodded.

No part of our trip could be called easy, but this was undoubtably our worst stretch. Moving constantly, we were swiftly reduced to exhausted, hungry, dispirited wanderers, not able to keep strictly to our eastward course. And the worst was yet to come.

It was in the waning hours of the day, as the sun glowed scarlet behind us, that we were finally forced to rest and pick over the meager offerings of two stunted "potato trees." Other than a little private banter among Jeff, Holly, and myself, there was no conversation. Chuck looked very worried.

We heard the massive animal slosh through the swamp toward us, but ignored it. Sheila had nicknamed the beasts "Samosaurs" because of their doggish heads, which reminded her of a pet she had once owned. They were at least forty feet long, including the stumpy dove tails, had three pairs of legs, the northernmost of which could be used for elementary grasping when the creature reared up on the hind pairs, and, of course, the enormous cocker spaniel heads with the six inch teeth.

Though they were obviously carnivorous, quite a number had stumbled by us during the day giving our group no more than token glances. So we got careless, and it cost us. As tired as we were, only Thumper looked up warily as another of the giants paused fifty yards from us, and he made no alarm. The beast stood and stared at us, its hairless blue head cocked to one side as if listening.

If only Shana hadn't stood at that moment and walked from the circle of the group, maybe the animal would have ambled on, looking for game elsewhere. But she had a cramp in her right leg and had to move around before it crippled her.

With her first couple of steps, the Samosaur jerked its head sharply in our direction. Its eye narrowed, considering this small, possible meal, and its quartered nose wrinkled hungrily. I took no notice, though as things turned out, there was nothing I could have done. Shana stopped and turned back to us to say something that was never said.

The Samosaurs were supposed to be dumb and slow, according to our scouting, but we had never seen one under the primordial impetus of attack. It literally launched itself through the mire at us with the speed of a cat and covered the intervening fifty yards in two blinks of an eye. Shana was instantly aware that she was the target, but the knowledge paralyzed her into a perfect quarry.

To give credit to the others, at least four of them were moving to her defense, but none of the men were near enough to help, and Shana was as good as dead. I really don't know how she thrust herself between the girl and that wide, lunging mouth, but, somehow, Sheila Roen knocked Shana out of the lethal path and substituted her own body.

The great jaws snapped shut on Sheila before she hit the ground, and her terrible scream of agony sliced through my consciousness like a freezing blade. The animal drew itself upward with its writhing catch, and the front legs left the muck defensively.

With a burst of hysterical energy, I leaped up and planted my feet on the ample lower gum, grasped the slick upper one between two teeth, and surged. I don't believe I had ever exerted my animal strength to its fullest before that moment, but I was too engrossed to feel surprise or triumph when the massive mouth began to open.

I heard the shouts from below through the hammering of blood in my ears; I heard them scream with exaltation and I heard them scream in horror. Two feet the jaws had parted, opening to release Sheila Roen, but I couldn't pull and avoid the swatting foreleg long enough to complete the job. The paw hit me hard and sent me spinning along a beautiful arc across the sky. I hit in four feet of water and two feet of mud.

As I struggled to the surface and gasped air, the lumbering monster turned away from us and, utilizing that unbelievable burst of speed, disappeared through the larger trees. The curtain-like moss parted and closed in passionless ease. My head bobbed above water just in time to hear the one last hopeless and forsaken wail.

I was shivering in the fading sunlight, but not from cold, even though I was still dripping wet from my fall. As I sat on comparatively dry ground with my knees drawn up under my chin and my arms around them, I shook constantly from pent up emotions, basically fear, sorrow, and rage. Holly was brushing down the fur on my shoulders and upper back, trying to warm and relax me, but I hardly noticed her.

Sheila was dead, of that there was no doubt, but the manner of her death and our own inability to prevent it ate at us like a malignant tumor. Chuck, Lew, Jeff, Hadji, and Bull were morosely silent, their faces long, dark masks; Linda was furiously whittling on more of her tiny arrows, occupying her mind; Doc and Mike were rather coldly calculating our chances of survival; and Shana was crying, just as she had been all evening.

7

"New Casper, Wyoming"

We were out of Dinosaur Swamp for six days, and our spirits, while not high, were back to the norm, if that was an improvement. We had just enough contact with scattered tribes to find that the intensive hunt for Shana was still in progress.

Shana simply endured our association, ate as alone as possible, and lived for the day when our small troop set foot on Earth once more. I had hinted broadly to Chuck on more than one occasion that her hatred and revulsion might eventually turn her against us if we ever did complete our journey. He, in turn, was counting on her having witnessed her father's death to force the truth to the proper people. I hoped he was right, because I was feeling some very peculiar opposing emotions toward this dark-haired, dishevelled beauty who regarded me as nothing more than a talking animal. Not the least of these emotions was strong physical attraction.

We'd stopped by the bank of a river to rest and swim. It was peaceful, but on Thear, one could not forget that every second there was the constant threat of danger. My acute senses had given me a kind of sixth awareness where danger was involved, either by sounds so quiet I never fully realized that I heard them, or smells so faint that I didn't know that they were triggering my suspicions. This sense, if it can be called such, interrupted my casual daydreaming then and woke my mind to the possibility of jeopardy. I surveyed both river banks but saw no noteworthy creature other than Shana, sitting where I had last seen her.

A sharp rattling from a tree above us snapped my eyes to attention and I saw a white flash heading straight for Shana's breast. I operate on two different reflex and perception levels, but I have to "switch gears" much like an automobile to the second level, which is about twice the speed of the average man's reactions. As I slipped into this overdrive, the white flash seemed to slow before my speeded up eyes until I recognized it as the long, headed shaft of an arrow. It was no more than six inches from her chest when I reached out and plucked it from the air.

Shana screamed and almost fainted. Throwing her to my shoulder, I leaped for the concealment of the forest, but was quickly stopped as four more arrows plunked into the dirt at my toes and another two buried themselves just behind my heels. I knew I couldn't catch all of the arrows from this many people, so I stood where I was and awaited developments.

"You in the river, out, and keep your hands up!" ordered a male voice from the trees.

Most of the others probably could have escaped by diving beneath the water and swimming downstream, but they had seen the display of archery and knew that Shana and I could look like giant porcupines in a matter of seconds. Not willing to risk her life, they complied, hands up.

The others of my group were dressing themselves as a number of new mutants, armed with crossbows, stepped from their concealment to look us over. Holly stood blushingly trying to cover herself until one of the more sympathetic of our captors shot her suit out of its tree with one arrow. They were good.

I stood Shana on the ground behind me and faced the men with hidden anger. I really didn't intend to be taken this easily, and waited for the opportunity to prove it.

"That's her, all right," said one of the men. "That hunting party we captured described her exactly." He was speaking of Shana.

A short boy with three well formed noses leered in agreement. "Lord, if them guys give us half a what they been promisin', it'll be hog heaven from here on in. Hey, Candy, you reckon maybe we could have a little fun from her and them other two girls before we turn 'em in?"

Candy, so named because he was lightly peppermint striped, nodded. "Heck, those troopers would settle just for her corpse, I'll bet."

Any wild, half-formed plans I had in my head were suddenly dissolved when I saw Jeff slowly fade from the scene at my right. The party that had captured us was so intensely interested in Shana, Ellen, and Holly that they failed to notice Nichols' vanishing act, an easy mistake since it involved no aggressive action or any movement at all. His camouflage was perfect. In fact, I could watch him only because I knew what to look for and anticipated his path as he walked silently forward. The sensors in his skin transmitted instructions on color and shadow, allowing him to blend into the background so effectively as to be virtually invisible.

The tallest and heaviest of our captors never knew what happened when Jeff swung a thick stick of wood at his crown and sent him crashing to the riverbank. The others reacted very unprofessionally as they glanced about to locate the disturbance. Though there were eleven of them, we had little trouble in overpowering them without any real bloodshed on either side.

The local patrol suddenly found the positions reversed as they picked themselves, unarmed, from the ground. "Oh brother," sighed the one known as Candy, "we're in for it now."

"That's right," Hadji said, "so don't make us do anything we don't absolutely have to."

I looked to Chuck for instructions.

So did Thumper. "Kill 'em?" he asked rather hopefully.

"No, don't kill, Thumper," Garner answered. "We'll let them guide us through this portion of the jungle. Later . . . well, we'll see then."

"Guide ya?" asked one of the boys. "You don't really think you can go right through the center of the city with us as hostages, do you?"

"What city?" inquired Jeff as he materialized.

"Whaddaya mean, 'what city'? New Casper, of course."

Chuck snorted, "Get serious, fella, New Casper's just a mythical piece of jungle gossip, and you know it."

"Like heck! I live there, we all do, and it's not more than an hour's walking distance," the other insisted.

I looked questioningly to Doc. He answered, "New Casper is supposedly the biggest mutant settlement on the continent. Campfire tales say it's a veritable New York City hidden from the troopers' raids by the dense trees overhead. It's named after a real town in Wyoming.

"Sure it is," Candy said, "and it's just east of here."

"Tell me another one," Finnegan muttered.

"But it's *there*! You would have run right into it."

Chuck looked vulnerable to some demonstrative persuasion, and I already believed in their story, though the concept of a large village growing without Earth interference was a little difficult to accept.

84

"Okay," said Chuck, "suppose you show us."

As corny as it sounds, my mouth did fall open when I first looked on New Casper, Wyoming, in the midst of a semi-tropical forest on Thear. For at least a mile in front of us, a thatched, mud hut city stretched out, its numerous double-storied buildings erected against the thick tree trunks, around them, and some even using two or more as corner posts. Clearly defined paths as wide as streets ran through the area in crisscrossing lanes, and a steady flow of human traffic, mostly women and toddlers, moved from house to house. This was a breathing city on a world where pitiful villages were blasted by Kurtz' sky troopers before any coherent form of civilization could evolve.

New Casper retained its shrouded state because the trees, rather than having been cleared, had been allowed to continue their unrestricted growth with their ceiling-like limbs concealing the life below. The shuttle craft seldom employed any means of detection other than visual sightings on their occasional scouting trips, so, with no artificial clearings or strips of cultivated land to signal them, they were highly likely to glide above the settlement in blissful ignorance of its existence. A sophisticated intelligence network worked out from New Casper informing the leaders of the goings and comings in the surrounding region. Our own arrival had proceeded us by at least thirty minutes.

The short man spoke, "Welcome to New Casper, Wyoming, ladies and gentlemen, if such you be. I am Albert Rosman Beasley, the Only, the founder of this veritable paradise, and your host—or jailer—for the duration of your stay here. Naturally, my official position is up to you and your conduct within the city limits."

Chuck smiled. "Don't worry, Mr. Beasley, our intentions are peaceful." He glanced at the cowed hunters who had forced our detour. "We're only passing through."

"I wasn't finished talking about myself," the founder of New Casper, Wyoming pointed out somewhat irritably. "I am presently twenty-five years old, have been an inmate of Thear for eleven years because I have a finned back and periodically belch clouds of turquoise gas, and have total control of the city and its inhabitants. You may wonder why these people, who so emphatically outnumber me, allow my dictatorial reign of debauchery to continue."

"No," Jeff admitted, "I haven't."

"It's because I make this place *work*. No other single freak on

85

this planet could take such a prize collection of foul-ups, drop-outs, and minus zeroes and produce a working, thriving community. It is with humble gratitude that I accept my loving followers' heartfelt praise and adoration.

"Right now, my weary friends, prepare yourselves to be received in grand fashion, New Casper fashion."

We were entertained with dances, acrobatics, anything the primal surroundings could offer. Food in abundant quantities was produced for our consumption, and we greedily accepted the roasted pig, beaver, and "woods cow" along with ripe fruit and less familiar cultivated green and red vegetables. A type of wine was brought to us, and I discovered its alcoholic potency after a single choking swallow. It was a good five times stronger than the weak beverage I had become accustomed to. Since I must admit that I have no head for strong drink, I stuck to water for the remainder of the meal.

The occasion was festive, and Beasley played his role to the hilt. He continually toasted us for the ingenuity, audacity, and selflessness of our plan to reach Earth, and, slightly drunk, pledged his life to its success. Yeah, things went fine until a rather bloodthirsty finale.

New Casper had its share of troublemakers and malcontents. While a predominantly fair system of laws were in existence concerning the minor areas of "thou shalt and shalt not," the Mayor himself presided over the more serious fractures of the social structure, and his proclamations were always final and zestfully given.

Beasley heard the claims against them first along with corroborating evidence, allowed them to speak briefly in their own defense, and passed sentence.

The first man was charged with murder and had a pretty substantial case against him, with four eyewitnesses. When allowed to speak, he sullenly muttered, "I got nothin' to say." Beasley practically laughed in glee as he pronounced the death penalty, execution of such to be immediate.

"Oh no, they're not going to kill him now, are they?" Holly whispered to me.

"Looks like," I replied with interest. I was a little worried about the reactions of guys like Thumper and Hadji, since they had been known to leap to the aid of single mutants assaulted by larger numbers. If the execution was swift and clean, perhaps they wouldn't do anything foolish.

Instead of flaming torches, his chosen executioner held nothing in his hands as he stepped from the shadows to perform his task. He surprised me by being a short, slender boy with green hair streaked with white, but his face showed delight as he prepared to carry out the order. For the first time, the doomed man broke from his quiet, surly character by struggling hysterically against his bonds when the boy approached him, but it was wasted energy.

"What's that little guy going to do?" asked Jeff in confusion. "Is he supposed to strangle him or something?"

Not knowing, I shrugged.

Beasley grinned and raised one hand before the two. "Let him *die*!" he said in a joyful tone.

The condemned prisoner moaned loudly through the gag while the other placed both hands on his forehead and began to grunt with growing effort. Suddenly a wave of aching pain hit my head, and I had to fight to keep from crying out before I abruptly lapsed into a waking dream of another time, another life.

In my mind, I stood at twilight outside a long, dark building with four doors that faced me. It was essential that I enter only by the single correct door, but my memory was tricking me, and I couldn't recall which was the way. Soon the sun would be completely below the distant hills and it would be too late...

"Oh, Eli," Holly was sniffing on my shoulder, "that's *horrible*!"

I shook my head and looked back at the execution scene. The man convicted of murder was dead, his head hanging loosely at his chest and a pair of large, black bruises on his forehead. But the other boy was still there, grinning, though somewhat tiredly.

"Excellent," boomed the Mayor. His applause ignited a whole river of clapping on either side of us, with accompanying shouts and whistles.

"What happened?" I said to Jeff, stunned.

"Weirdest thing I ever saw," he answered in a marvelling voice. "The guy just shivered all over and *wilted*. A truly weird occurrence."

"Next, next!" demanded a whetted Beasley.

The bound girl was seized under the arms and lifted to face her accusers. Her eyes were as wide with fright as a spooked doe's.

"The little wench is charged with stealing penned pigs, most high judge," declared an appointed speaker melodramatically. "A serious charge, indeed."

"Yes," nodded Beasley with false gravity.

"Remove the gag. Are you guilty or innocent, girl?"

Coughing, she shook her head. "Honestly, I never took any animals! I didn't steal anything from anyone, Mayor! Some men came to my hut and placed me under arrest without saying why or letting me explain—"

Beasley interrupted her, "What is your name?"

"Patricia, sir, Patricia—"

"Well, then, Patricia, all you have to do is prove your innocence by telling us where you were when the theft took place. Providing witnesses, of course."

Her voice was low and meek. "I was alone, Mayor, in my hut. I haven't mated yet, and I live with no one else."

"That's not an overwhelming defense, Patricia," Beasley pointed out. "I'm afraid I must pronounce you guilty. Punishment will be transference."

"No! God, no, please! I didn't do anything!" she wailed to him. "Please, please!"

A piece of wadding was re-inserted into her mouth and strapped tightly in place by a strip of animal hide.

The previous executioner watched the proceedings with smiling eyes and waved to two of his own flunkies who appeared carrying a caged pig between them. The girl was strapped to the same post as before.

"Not again," hissed Jeff. "You can't murder a kid for stealing a pig she may not have even stole!"

"*You* tell them," I said. But I was ready to stand.

The boy didn't kill this one, however. Having the pig raised to shoulder level by his men, he reached through the bamboo-like bars and grasped it roughly by its pink snout. The fat, hairless little animal squealed and tried to break free, but the boy held on tightly. Next he grabbed a large handful of straight, dark hair on the convicted girl's head and began snorting and trembling once more.

The pain and nausea rolled over me again, but I fought it back this time and viewed the operation with clear eyes. To most of the others of my group, it must have looked like he was merely torturing the madly struggling girl and the now quiet pig, but I had a good idea just what type of mental powers this mutant held and how much of the impossible was within his means. Beasley had said "transference," not death.

I heard Beasley's breathy exhortations as he leered like some crazed child at the spectacle. The girl twisted violently against the ropes and choked on the tight gag, as she tried desperately to scream, but slowly she began to calm. Like a dying flame, her struggles lessened in a gradual curve until her breathing was regular and her eyes were almost closed. For a moment, everything, including the girl and the animal, was silent.

"Thank goodness," Holly whispered. "I was afraid he was going to kill her."

Abruptly, like an exploding sun, the pig started to squeal. They were long, high screams that were lost on the rest of my party, but for me they were as clear as the last page in a book. The unbelievable power and range of the executioner's mind sent me recoiling. The animal literally threw itself against the bamboo bars of the cage in a blind hysteria.

"The punishment," shouted Beasley, "is complete!"

A thousand voices joined his in a tremendous cheer that signalled the end to the ceremony proper, leaving only the mopping up to be done. Beasley grandly awarded the "remaining hull of this unfortunate thief" to the young executioner to do with what he wished.

"Where're you going, Cat?" Jeff asked, as I stood.

"Got to talk to a man about something," I answered without answering and walked away.

Around me, the uproarious feast had resumed in all its stereophonic glory, but the men holding the pig were still conferring with one another. The animal itself was now lying on the cage floor, trembling and moaning.

"What'll we do with her?" the executioner was saying as I approached.

"She's Rouark's," replied Beasely. "Let him take her to replace the missing pigs. He can have her for Sunday dinner or keep her for a pet for all I care."

I marched grimly up to him. "I want to talk to you," I announced.

He looked around. "Oh, yes, you're one of the pilgrims, aren't you? The one they call . . . Lion?"

"Cat," I corrected, "and I think what you just did to that poor kid is the most disgusting thing I ever saw in my entire life, and, brother, I've seen a lot."

A look of annoyance passed over his features. "You forget yourself, Cat. After all, you are only a guest here and have little right to question our methods of discipline." A sudden, benign smile replaced the annoyance. "Now go, enjoy. The food is abundant, the women are soft, please take advantage of my hospitality."

"You've got to be kidding," I spat. "What about Patricia?"

"Yes? What about her? She doesn't seem to be in any discomfort to me." He gestured to the slack-jawed, dull-eyed shell that stood emptily, held erect by the ropes.

"That's nothing more than a zombie, you bastard. What about *her*!" I pointed to the crying animal thing in the cage.

I had stepped a little too hard, as Beasley's clouding expression told me, and his voice was like dry ice. "Don't you ever take such liberties with a man such as myself again. Yuri, explain it to our friend."

The boy nodded.

An invader, an alien was suddenly in my brain. He barged in like some rampaging elephant and lay bare the private recesses of my soul, as I screamed out in pain and terror. It was *wrong*! No one could come in, no one could—

Instinctively, I lashed out with a bolt of hatred at the slender death dealer who faced me and watched as his countenance was shocked into a mask of fear. "Oh my God!" he cried out. *"Oh God!"* And he fled into the night.

Beasley's own face was startled. "How did you...unless you're...guards! Kill him! Now!"

Three men quickly responded to his command, but I was a bit faster than all of them, punching the first in the mouth, kicking the second in the groin, and shoving the third into his followers.

"Kill him!" Beasley screamed in a blue panic.

I was swarmed under by unarmed men and almost brought to the ground, but then Thumper was beside me, and we began to clear the area. Bodies flew like bowling pins as we punched, kicked, and clawed our way out of the rushing tide. But Beasley was their leader, their Mayor, and they obeyed him like slaves, always pressing forward to meet our slashing attack. Suddenly Bull was with us, and then Doc. Ellen appeared at my side, followed by Jeff and Hadji. Lew was a whirling devil, and Finnegan laughed out his battle cry above the din of screams and curses. Mike hit the living wall like a bulldozer and cleared us a passage through blood and broken bones.

"The river!" Chuck shouted to us.

I saw Holly grab Linda and run as if the hounds of Hell were nipping at her legs, which is also an apt description of how Beasley turned tail when he saw that his henchmen wouldn't be able to immediately stop us.

But we also knew that we couldn't hope to overcome a thousand maniacal villagers, so we drove for Chuck's goal, the river, and the tiny, concealed harbor that New Casper, Wyoming had erected there.

Almost incredibly, we made the river without suffering any serious wounds and found the dock as if led by a guide. It was being watched by a couple of warriors who were obviously upset at being excluded from the celebration and were well on the way to remedying matters with a jug of eighty proof. Jeff grinned maliciously as he faded into invisibility and crept forward.

"Best wumman I ever had," one guard was slurring to the other. "Trained ever muscle in her body."

The other nodded solemnly, and his eyes widened in bloodshot awe when the heavy jug seemed to float out of his limp hands and smash down on his abruptly unconscious cranium. The first drinker watched this in belch-broken silence before he spat off the deck into the river and said with bruised feelings, "If thass all you got to say, then stuff it," and fell noisily asleep.

I was laughing uncontrollably as Jeff blinked back into existence with a puzzled look on his face. "Can you beat that?" he said wonderingly. "I didn't even touch him."

Then Chuck reminded us that we had little time for levity and hustled us onto one of the six log rafts. The floats were a good twenty feet by twenty feet, held together by vine lashings and a natural form of sap paste, and had a rude, but workable rudder on each. Long slender poles were bound to their sides.

"They'll just follow us," Shana said in a defeated voice, "and you know they have more experience at this than we have. They'll catch us."

"Not necessarily," Mike grunted. He walked to the nearest raft and, his great back bulging, ripped it loose of its moorings. It slid quietly into the inky water and, once caught by the sluggish tide near the center, glided slowly into the night.

"Bright," Hadji laughed. He and I helped to free the others.

Horace, who had kept himself stationed in the trees near the bank, came skittering back toward us, screaming in a hysterical whisper, "They're coming, a posse, they're almost here!"

"Onto the raft, bright boys," Chuck ordered, and we waded over to the rest.

The six strongest were put to work on the poles, and we drove the spinning craft out to the center of the river with divergent, but roughly compatible strokes against the soft bottom. Chuck shouted for Jeff to man the rudder, and the latter did so with the utmost reluctance.

"Just wait until we've got the raft facing east—that's with the current—and then hold it straight back," Garner told him.

"I've always had trouble with mechanical things," Jeff muttered.

"I know what you mean," I added, indicating the pole I held.

The villagers clustered along the bank in a long, torch-lit line and hurled futile obscenities at us. These inhabitants of what was probably Thear's only non-government-erected city still rallied around their cruel, tyrannical, and supercilious leader and threw their curses and abuse through the night air. One man, who looked like he belonged in the water anyway, swam after us like some angered dolphin, but Finnegan turned him back with a well-timed shot in the mouth that left several teeth embedded in the pole.

Pursuit was useless, and we were beyond effective arrow range, so the glaring torches were soon no more than matches flickering in the distance. But something inside me hurt deeply with the revelations of the night. Our own could be as cruel and merciless as the normal humans, I had seen the power of a mutant mind condemn Patricia to a living hell for as long as her life might extend, and, worst of all, I had felt the depths of fear in unleashing the unknown abilities of my own brain. It scared me. Bad.

"Look at them," Jeff said quietly. "Who are the fools among us?"

"Eli," came Holly's softly trembling voice at my ear. She slipped my free arm around her shoulders, and I rubbed her reflexively. "Why did they hate us so much just because you tried to help that poor little girl?"

She still didn't know; none of them did. "I can't say, Holly. Maybe I just interfered at the wrong time."

"Yeah," agreed Jeff with a smile, "I can't take you anywhere."

8

"Assault on a Space Port"

"We should have come this route to begin with," declared Hadji early the next morning as Capella birthed itself ahead of us. "With that good current we finally caught, I'll bet we've covered fifty miles from 'New Loonieland' back there."

Ellen lovingly ran her long-nailed hands through his curly black hair. She was a tall, lanky, awkwardly pretty girl, a veteran of eleven years on Thear because of her claw-like nails and what Hadji considered to be a "delightful" two foot tail where tails are supposed to be.

Hadji and Ellen made an unlikely-looking pair, if Thear offered anything like a well-matched pair. She was, as I said, tall and slim, but he, though even taller, looked stocky and broad in comparison. His eyes said Oriental, but the curl in his hair contradicted this, and his skin was East Indian dark. His mutant badge was an armor-like covering around his chest and back. Chuck would have had to have taken them both, even if either one hadn't been a superb fighter, because one simply would not have gone without the other.

Laying Holly aside as lightly as possible, I found Chuck at the bow of the craft that had rescued us the night before. I had taken the expected dressing-down in private for angering our hosts. Garner had been quiet, but strong in his criticism, and I think I confounded him by taking it in level silence. I could have thrown up some sort of defense by telling him what I knew about Patricia, but I didn't feel at that time that there was any reason for explanations.

Though I had no intense need to be chastised, I sought out Chuck because of the deep frown that spread its way across the whole of his face. I sat uninvited at his side and said, "Problems?"

He breathed a tired sigh before replying, "I could peddle 'em wholesale."

"I tried to be good, so what's the matter?"

"Aside from our inglorious expulsion from New Casper, I'm not even sure if this river will carry us within a hundred miles of the port, my stomach is almost as stable as a roller coaster, and *she's* worse than ever," he told me, hanging a thumb in the direction of the right (starboard?) side of the raft.

Huddled there in an almost fetal position was Shana Wilbanks, her back turned to us and her entire body shaking with soundless sobs.

"Been like that for eight hours," he informed me.

"How come?"

"Our old friend Finnegan. He's ... well, you know, he's elemental. When he's hungry, he eats, when he's angry, he fights. When he needs a woman ..."

It dawned on me, heavily.

"Those dancers had him pretty well worked up before we had to ... leave last night, and Finnegan needed somebody badly. He knew you wouldn't let him near Caribou, and, though he doesn't fear them, he's got respect for Hadji *and* Ellen, and Linda, ah, well. So that only leaves Shana ..."

I clucked my tongue. "Knowing Shana's personal opinion of any and all mutants, I'd have to guess he raped her."

"She's got bruises on her face the size and shape of his open hand. Told her he'd break her neck if she even moaned."

I glanced at the unworried, snoozing form of the long Irishman. "What do you want me to do? Beat him up?"

"That wouldn't do any good. But it's Shana I'm worried about. I'm afraid that, even if we make it back to Earth, she will refuse to help us."

"She saw those 'loyal patriots of Earth' beat her own father to death."

"And has she fared much better with us? The Throwbacks try to eat her, a dinosaur almost does, Finnegan rapes her, and your advances aren't much more civilized."

"You see everything, don't you? My fragile ego thanks you from the bottom of its depraved little heart."

He ignored me. "Why should she help us? Haven't we been the animals she expected?"

I spoke purposely loudly so she might also hear. "I don't think you need to worry, Chuck. I'm sure that Shana realizes she has to gain the protection of whatever rational Congressmen remain, or she'll be as dead as the rest of us."

"I hope you're right. Still I wish we could do something for her."

"I'll talk to her," I said.

"No, she won't let anyone near her, especially not men."

"Maybe Holly, then."

"Okay, Cat, see what she can do for us."

I was cut short by the delirious outcry of an adult elephant, or what sounded like one. "Hot damn!" Bull Mumbali shouted. "This is it, Chuck, this is the place!"

"The space port?" asked Garner, peering at the unbroken foliage on both banks.

"Not fifteen miles from it!" he declared. "Before I was relocated, I worked all the farms in this area, and there's one just around the bend. We'd better get off this tub, or we'll be sitting ducks."

As we grabbed the long poles and dug them deeply into the bottom, a new vigor flowed through our muscles; it was joy, anticipation, and some fear. We were practically to the point that at least half of us had never really expected to see, and, except for two, we were alive and our plans were intact. Hadji almost had to pull Ellen from a pole she had insisted on manning and, as old hat as it sounds, someone began singing. It wasn't me, but I would have if I could carry notes in a fifty gallon drum.

We did everything slowly that day. The reason for this was twofold: first, Bull had to take a reasonable amount of time to reawaken old memories of the surrounding jungle, and, secondly, Chuck wanted to attack the port only after dark, which was understandable.

Eating when we felt like it, we moved still eastward through the wilderness, avoiding Farms and any other populated areas where an advance alarm might be sounded. I had briefly run down Shana's problem to Holly, and she was as sorrowfully empathetic as I had expected, but not as successful in consoling the victimized girl as I had hoped. While she couldn't elicit much therapeutic conversation from Shana, she wasn't, at least, driven away and hovered protectively about her all day.

We encountered the outer gates of Earth Space Port One about two hours before sundown and spent the remaining light discreetly reconnoitering. Bull assured us that the four shuttle craft and one messenger ship on the wide landing pad to the south side were far below the total usually kept there in non-unloading periods, which meant that the local Kurtz flunkies were indeed still out desperately searching for the girl who could bring political ruin on the present system. And this was after two months.

They didn't expect that same girl to be standing outside the very gates that protected them from the outside world, and this left us full of fight and confidence. Bull and Finnegan were ready to tackle the outfit barehanded. As usual, I was having second thoughts.

Darkness fell just as we assembled in a well-grown patch of land outside the main gate's control building. Bull told us that the building held at least six trained men who monitored all portions of the highly-charged fence electronically and that only suited troopers could have the doors swung open to admit them. We had to get past this obstacle just to have a shot at stealing a ship.

"I think I can get in."

"Eli, that fence is fifteen feet high and there aren't any trees near it," Holly said worriedly.

"I know, believe me, but I still think I can get past the gate."

"What then?" asked Chuck.

"I play it by ear, get in the control building somehow, and open it for the rest of you."

"Sounds easy enough to me," Jeff said. "In fact, if it weren't for this severe case of gout I'm experiencing, I'd love to go along with you."

"I'm flattered," I replied. "Well, are you willing to let me try? At worst, I'll get my block shot off and you'll have to find another way in."

"If he really thinks he can do it, I'm all for him," said Mike.

I left them there and made my way through the jungle to a point some three or four hundred yards down, figuring that this part of the fence—though as brightly lit as the rest—might not be as closely monitored as the main entrance. It might be to my advantage, I reasoned, if those inside didn't observe my means of entrance.

To the deep west, silent lightning flickered ominously, reminding me of the brutal energy coursing through the metal fence rising before me. Holly was no eye-judge of heights or distances. The fence was actually twenty feet high and topped with four strands of barbed wire, but it was no lower elsewhere, so I began to mentally prepare myself. Just twenty feet, maybe nineteen, nothing, nothing at all . . .

A twig snapped behind me, and I spun about, my flared nostrils feeling for smells. She was no more than ten feet away, hidden in some shrubs. "Come on out, Holly," I said somewhat wearily.

She stepped into the clearing with a sheepish look on her features and head bowed. "I just...wanted to watch," she explained.

"Why not? It may be one big, spectacular fish fry," I muttered.

Her eyes darted up. "Be careful, Eli, *please*!"

"Hey, don't worry about that. I've sort of grown to like me."

Her voice was a trembling whisper. "I *love* you, Eli."

I didn't know what to say. I realized I should respond by saying I loved her, too, but I couldn't. I didn't.

Awkwardly, I reached out and brushed the thick blond hair from her right cheek, touched it for a moment, and said, "You do, don't you?" Could one be more modestly eloquent than that?

She said nothing.

"Now get back in the trees; you might be seen."

She left.

I've always felt that if my body size had corresponded closely to my outsized strength, I would have weighed over a ton, and, though pulling only a hundred and sixty improved my agility immeasurably, this lack of mass had hurt me on various occasions. Too often, I had had to "plant" myself solidly on the ground by external means to gain full advantage of my muscles. But this definitely was not a time when I regretted weighing as little as I did.

Taking one last, frightened look at the fence, I muttered, "Aw, hell, I'm not going to *think* myself across," and launched a long-strided run into the bare area before the fence. Some fifteen yards away, I bunched my legs and sprang upward.

Twenty feet is a long way, especially up. The last world record broad jump mark was only ten or so feet longer than that, and the high jump mark was well under half as much, but I had leaped with all of my energy and sailed through the violet night sky while approaching light flashes burst in the distance. Sweating, praying, and shaking, I cleared the uppermost strand of barbed wire by at least five feet.

The trip down was beautiful, until I slammed into a forced roll on the bare earth on the opposite side. I was inside and not the first angry warning bell had clanged or the first searchlight split the darkness. A low rumbling did break the silence, but it was only thunder. As I stood, uninjured, I thought I heard a muffled voice call out, "Way to go, Cat."

Okay, big shot, I thought, so you're inside, now what? Though I could probably have forced my way into the foreboding black building that faced me from behind the glaring floodlights, such a post would undoubtedly have contained sophisticated warning alarms, and I hadn't come this far to stop a bullet, which is a bit more difficult to catch than an arrow. It was a situation requiring a more cerebral form of attack.

Well, it had worked for the Greeks and a numberless collection of historical imitators, so why not give it a try? In spite of the fact that I really didn't look like a wooden horse, I strolled toward the brightest spot before the entrance to the building, eliciting, I'm sure, confused expletives from my hidden companions.

I got as close as ten feet from the huge double doors before a short burst of automatic gunfire mutilated the dirt just beyond my curled up toes. "Friend!" I shouted as loudly as possible. "Kamerad! White Flag! Amigo!"

A deep metallic voice boomed back from somewhere in the structure, "Remain stationary and identify yourself."

"Elias Harper!" I answered. "Mutant, number...uh...V1185302. I've got some news about that girl, what's her name, Wilbanks?"

The loudspeaker gave no hint, but I'm sure they registered surprise. Finally, the voice said, "Affirmative. Computer check reveals number V118-5302 as Harper, Elias Blaine, male, Caucasian. How were you admitted to this compound?"

"Oh," I said brightly, "I went through the fence."

"Explain."

"The way everyone does. Let me in and I'll show you."

"Deferred. What information do you have of Shana Wilbanks?"

"I know where she is." That should draw a bite.

"Where?"

"Let me in and I'll tell you everything you want to know."

There was a short silence which I attributed to those inside holding a quick conference. Then my answer came. "Place both of your palms firmly atop your head and do not remove them. At the signal, walk slowly toward the door in front of you, making no sudden or obscured moves."

I tried to suppress a smile as I lay my hands on my head.

"Proceed."

The doors swung out, and I marched from the rapidly clouding night into the flourescent brilliance of the receiving room. I stood in this featureless, eight-foot cubicle until whatever detection devices were operating were satisfied that I was unarmed, and then I strolled from there into a larger room when the door slid back. It was obviously the main control center.

I tried to blink innocently in the light, while actually observing the wall-sized panels of closed circuit TV screens and glowing lights. Six fatigue-dressed troopers were assembled to meet me, and I felt sure that this was the entire remaining outer security guard. Three of the men were armed with projectile style hand weapons, and one carried a stunner.

"You may lower your arms," one of the troops told me.

"Thanks, sir," I replied as I shook them in apparent discomfort. "I ain't been any too healthy since I got the fever, and even a little strain can..."

Five of them flinched at my mention of a "fever," but the man who had spoken to me grinned at them. Then he said, "You claim to know the whereabouts of Shana Wilbanks, is that right?"

"Right as rain, sir. I seen 'er with my own two eyes. I only got two, not like some of those freaks out there—"

"You're not here to talk about your deformities or lack of them!" snapped another man, an armed one. "Where is she?"

"Well, now, that seems to be my only ace in the hole, don't it? I'm not greedy, mind you. I'm willing to bargain for reasonable stakes: a good, hot meal, a night's sleep in a bed—"

"Bargain hell!" the second man barked. "If you don't speak up right now, I'll put a bullet between your filthy eyes and dump your body for the carrion pickers!"

"Didn't mean to upset you so, mister," I drawled.

The first man came to my defense, sort of. "Take it easy, Jeptha, he's obviously very slow. I don't think a good meal and bed are too much for him to ask."

"And them other things you guys promised," I broke in.

One of the others didn't feel as generous. "Let's make him talk now or kick him out for what he is, a conniver."

"Calm down, he's just a simple—"

The second man interrupted, "Simple, my eye. Let's shoot some truth serum into him and have done with it." The rest muttered agreement.

"Isn't that a little drastic?" my defender inquired.

"Shubert, every hour Wilbanks is out there alive is a new threat to Director Kurtz and the Empire," another, older man said. "I'm sorry, but I have to agree with the others. We should pry the information out as soon as possible."

The first man looked at me and shrugged. "Sorry, old boy," he said, "I tried."

"Lord, Lord, what's going to happen to me?" I commiserated with beautiful terror.

"Just a little show and tell session," replied a man with a gun, as he took my arm and led me into a corridor. "Like where Shana is and how you got past the gates."

I was taken to a smaller room a few doors down and placed on a long, narrow table. The only man who had accompanied me was the one with the gun, but I figured the rest would be along once they thought the looselips juice was rolling around in my veins. My captor strapped me to the table with adjustable leather bands across my calves, waist, wrists, and neck.

Once he had me secured, he holstered the gun and even buttoned the flap, forseeing no personal danger. He appropriated a long syringe from a glass-faced cabinet and prepared a slightly bluish solution to fill it. Spouting a couple of drops to force out all of the remaining air, he smiled and approached me.

"There's really not much pain involved," he assured me.

I waited until he bent over my left forearm to administer the dose and then ripped my hand free of the thin bond and, before he could react, tore the gun, holster and all, from him and tossed it away. He tried to scream and run, but I rapped him lightly across the temple, and he collapsed in open-mouthed unconsciousness.

"Sweet dreams," I said.

Quickly snapping the other straps, I freed myself and laid his sleeping body on the table, covered by a crisp, white sheet so the deception wouldn't be too obvious. Once the gun was safely in my possession, I leaned against the wall by the single door and waited, passing the time by idly whistling.

No more than five minutes went by before I heard the sound of a lone pair of footsteps coming down the hall toward my room.

"Hey, Charlie," called a voice from the corridor, "is he ready yet?"

I kept silent, and he continued to speak. "How long is that stuff good for? I'd like to hear first hand if some of those weird sex-rites tales are true." He opened the door and stepped in. "Charlie?"

"They're stranger than fiction," I answered, popping Jeptha, the second man in the control center, on the back of the head. I caught him carefully as he fell, disarmed him, and laid him on the floor next to his partner.

The intercom system was located on the wall by the door, and, whistling again, I pressed the button marked "Control Room" and waited. Presently, a voice spoke, "Yeah?"

"Some of you guys better get in here and listen to what this gawf's saying. You won't believe it."

"Be right there," replied an eager voice.

This time the sounds of their feet told me that two more were coming, but I was still a little disappointed. I had hoped that all four would hurry in and ease my burden. The pair walked in as casually as the previous fellow, and I gently relieved them of their senses, acquiring a stunner in the process of search and seizure. This did mean, however, that at least one gun was yet in the possession of the other men.

So, Mohammad goes to the mountain.

I was out in the hall, highly exposed, before the intercom began to call for an answer from the men in the interrogation room. I knew he would get suspicious when none came, but I hoped that it would take a little longer before he tried to investigate. I was halfway to the control room, without a sign of cover, when the door began to open.

If he had a gun, I was dead.

Glancing wildly around—I had stupidly forgotten to bring one of the purloined weapons with me— I finally thought to look up and noticed the suspended or "lay-in" ceiling tile there. For its installation, a metal grid system is hung and the two by four sheets of tile are dropped into place from the area above. Taking a chance, I leaped up next to the wall, knocked one sheet up and out, and caught a precarious hold at the top of that same wall. Hauling the rest of me through the opening, I was effectively hidden in the dark space just below the insulated roof.

There was this gaping eight square foot hole in the corridor's ceiling, but, like any other person, the man walked right down the hallway without gazing up enough to notice. I was still whistling almost inaudibly as he passed directly beneath my hiding place with his gun drawn. I dropped softly to his shoulders and thumbed him out.

One other man waited beyond the light metal door, the only one to vote against my involuntary interrogation, and I was reasonably sure he didn't have a gun. I smashed the door open with one solid kick and dodged a three foot length of galvanized pipe that was swung a bit too quickly.

Leaning casually against the corridor wall, I watched as he sprang into the doorway, both hands raised for another strike at my head. He paused before leaping at me. A slow, defeated smile crossed his lips.

"Nope," I said, pointing to the pipe.

"Drop it?" he asked.

"Right."

The pipe clattered to the floor, and the man looked bemusedly at his newly empty hands. "Do you intend to beat me up?"

I shook my head. "No reason. I will, however, have to tie you up."

"That's reasonable. By the way, I'm Jack Shubert."

We shook, and I used some rubber coated electrical wire to bind him securely to one of the console chairs that were bolted before the control panel. He calmly indicated which lever operated the main gate and was intelligent enough not to pull a cross on me.

I watched the primary monitor as the huge gates parted inward and the first heavy drops of a thunder storm plopped to the ground. Again Shubert assisted me by revealing the controls to the loudspeaker.

Smugly satisfied, I electronically announced, "It's midnight and time for all the coachmen to change back into rats and all the bats to field mice. That ought to cover every one of you bums, so come on in; the weather's better in here."

Though fully dressed in civilized clothing for the first time in over a year, I still felt practically naked as I fidgeted uneasily in the deep green troop uniform.

"Can you please hold still?" Holly giggled. She was padding the shoulders of the slightly oversized jacket with torn fabric from others.

"It doesn't *feel* right," I said irritably.

"What's the matter, Bald Shoulders? Miss the sound of little fleas' feet running around your personal forest?" Jeff verbally jabbed at me. He was already dressed in his stolen uniform, not having had my problem of removing incriminating excess hair.

An unfamiliar stinging sensation coated my shoulders, back, and arms from their first shave in months, and, as hackneyed as it may sound, my feet hurt in the large shoes. Jeff, Finnegan, Lew, and I were disguised as Kurtz "employees" in hopes that we could effectively bluff our way with eleven mutant "captives" through a blinding rain halfway across the inner compound to the landing field. There, with Bull's help and direction, we hoped to hijack a ship back to Earth.

I was eventually outfitted well enough to suit Holly's stringent eye, and the three guns and one stunner were allotted to us in order to make it more official in appearance. Only Finnegan had ever handled and fired a pistol, but I had practiced with a citizen caliber stunner, so I opted for that weapon. Lew and Jeff were shown how to operate their guns' safeties and advised to leave them in the "on" position by Chuck, who had some experience in the area.

"There's no sense in our killing one another," he pointed out, "because we'll have plenty of competition in that endeavor."

"Awright you buzzards, line up and do it now!" Jeff shouted, waving his gun above his head.

"Will you watch that?" Chuck hissed. "Finnegan, you and Lew lead this little delegation, Bull can walk behind you and give directions. The rest of us will group together, and Jeff and Cat will guard our rear."

"Typecast again," I sighed.

Checking our bound prisoners (only Shubert was conscious), we resolutely strode out through the *front* door.

Thunder rumbled like the indigestion of the gods and was accompanied by eye-dazzling bolts of lightning. We counted on the inclement weather to help us make our way through the middle of the troop-filled compound without incident. Bull had assured us that the sight of a number of selected mutants being transferred from one building to another was not unusual in this interrogation-prone area. He also said that we could count on finding a fuelled, ready for launch communications ship waiting for us, since that was the fastest form of contact available. Supralight speeds left radio and kindred methods far behind.

We were led through the alternately black and silver night down streets of acrylic sheathing and past long, dark buildings like winding pythons. We weren't challenged, though several lone troops passed us at respectable distances, until we approached the actual landing area. There a single, miserable guard waited in a small booth erected at the gates to allow us passage, or refuse it.

"Papers," he said boredly as Lew halted us.

"We have to get these prisoners inside," Chang told him in an authoritative voice. "Green light orders."

The guard coughed and leaned out through the open door of the booth. "I don't give a damn if you have to teach them ballet, nobody gets through without specific papers signed by the comptroller or accompanying the comptroller himself."

Lew turned to his left and smiled. "That," he said above the rumbling weather, "is just too bad." His right leg shot out at an almost impossible angle, and his foot clipped the man's jaw. "Too bad," he repeated while the unconscious guard slipped to the floor.

Finnegan reached into the booth and opened the gates.

"Fourth ship," Bull pointed out for us. "It's bigger than the shuttles. Built for speeds greater than transfer ships, but it can handle twenty or more."

"Hell, let's quit talking and get to it," Finnegan spat.

No one was on the field, probably because the total unmolestation of years past had made them lax in security. After all, who would believe that a group of fourteen mentally inferior mutants and one unskilled normal girl could infiltrate such a well-defended outpost or attempt to steal a government interstellar communications vehicle? But, of course, though we were in a position to try that, our path was not strewn with roses. Arriving at the ramp leading up to the coin-shaped craft, Bull stopped Lew and Finnegan from marching blithely up to what might have been their (and our) deaths.

"You lay a hand on that door and this place will be drowning in gun-toting troops faster than you can sneeze," he warned them.

Jeff glanced at me. "I can sneeze pretty fast."

"How do we get in?" Lew asked.

"There's a panel down there on the ramp with six English letters followed by three numbers. They change the combination every night."

"Great," Chuck muttered. "If you try the wrong combination, I suppose it sets off the alarm?"

"No, I don't think so."

"Maybe that's a break. Doc?"

The only four-armed and broken-spectacled young man I've ever seen look scholarly in a thunderstorm left his place in the group and walked up to them.

"Since you've got that photographic memory, do you think you can keep trying different combinations and get us into this thing?" asked Chuck.

"Well, the permutations involved with such a variety of factors might prove difficult to—"

"Can you do it?" Garner snapped.

"Of course. But it will take time, perhaps hours."

"Then get to it. The rest of you can get your hands down and try to look inconspicuous. Go over behind the ramp."

Doc spoke to Bull. "Can the pattern include numbers alternating with letters?"

"Nope. Just a couple of the six letters followed by any three numbers."

"That reduces the variables significantly. Actually, two of the letters will probably be more likely to predominate due to a peculiarity of human reasoning and selectiveness. 'A' and—"

"Will you please get started?" Chuck almost shouted.

So we sat down, in the rain, with nature's fireworks on display all about us, and waited. But not for long. With blissful ignorance, a single Kurtz trooper came striding down the flooding street towards a point that would have been past our position and, thus, would have revealed us in our incriminating incongruity. I started to rise and have an attempt at bluffing my way into his acquaintance and giving him some excellent reason for not passing, but Finnegan, who was closer to the street, beat me to his feet.

"Oh, God," Chuck whispered, "he'll blow everything."

I listened, straining my ears to filter out the distractions of the storm. Finnegan approached the other man casually enough, even smiling with affected good humor, and when they came together, both stopped as if it were an actual chance meeting.

"Good evening, Captain," said the new man, recognizing Finnegan's bars as superior to his own. "Evil night, isn't it?"

"Damn shitty night," Finnegan replied. "Where are you headed?"

"Shuttle seven. I've got night duty this evening. We're going to take another run about the 'L' section looking for that girl. Although I don't see why—"

Finnegan laughed. "Where've you been for the last six hours?"

"Been, sir?"

"That's right. I don't stutter."

"Why, uh, in my bunk, sir."

"Then you haven't heard?"

"Heard, sir?"

"That Wilbanks bitch was found before nightfall," Finnegan improvised. "Her and eighteen of her freak friends were shot to death about a hundred miles west of here."

The other grinned. "That's certainly good news. She could have made it rough on all of us if she'd talked to the wrong people."

"That's right."

"By your leave, sir, I'll just be getting back to my bunk. I've been on twenty hour duty for almost a week now."

Finnegan, for no understandable reason, shook his head and said, "That's what you think, sucker." Then he kneed the man in the groin.

The trooper doubled over in screaming agony, drawing his gun by reflex. Before he could aim it, Finnegan chopped sharply down on the exposed back of his neck and snapped it like a stick of candy.

As the dead man fell, the gun went off loudly enough to be distinguished over the thunder.

"What the hell are you doing?" demanded Chuck, leaping to his feet.

"Repaying some old debts," Finnegan smiled, "with interest."

"He was *leaving*, you damned fool!"

The Irishman's dark eyes hardened. "Don't call me that."

"Then shut up and get over here!" This was the most Garner had ever dared with Finnegan, but his anger drove him on. "And pray that no one heard that shot."

Naturally, someone did. She was a WAC, or whatever equivalent Kurtz' army contained, and she came out of the pouring darkness calling for "Johnny," undoubtedly the dead man. With ice cold resolve, Finnegan pulled his own gun, aimed through the veil-like rain, and shot her through the left breast, killing her instantly. Too many people heard that shot.

Lights were suddenly flaring on all over the field, and the lightning paled in their brilliance. Along with the spotlights came the softer glows from the barracks inside the gates, signalling to us that our troubles were only beginning. Doc was working furiously at the panel, punching in new letter-number combinations with each of his hands, but, as yet, the doors remained closed and uncaring. We heard the gates to the field opening.

"Spread out!" Chuck shouted. "Away from the ship! Not you, Doc!"

I understood; we were to use ourselves as decoys while Starett, inexpendable at this point, continued looking for the right pattern of letters and numbers. I practically lifted a stumbling Holly to her feet and darted out into the now blindingly lit open with my stun ray set at maximum range and effectiveness. Someone shouted to me from the direction of the gate, but no shots were fired, probably because of my uniform.

Bull wasn't so lucky. Still dressed only in his mutant trunks, his massive, but twisted body and arms were displayed for all to see, and someone upfield did. The shot cracked in the night like something breaking, and Mumbali roared and clutched at his shoulder. Spinning like some grotesque ballerina, Bull slammed to the ground with an audible expulsion of air from his lungs and lay jerking spasmodically.

I slid to my side on the wet street, as I tried to reverse direction, and, to cover my mistake, I sprayed out a wide blue swath of stunning energy in the still-darkened area from which the shot had come. Cries told me I scored at least two hits, but I wasn't terribly interested in this while I broke into a jagged run to where Bull lay.

He was conscious, and great waves of red blood rolled from his nose and mouth across his dark face. They'd hit a lung.

"Ain't this the shaft?" he sputtered. "I come two thousand frigging miles to get to this place and as soon as my worth's over, bam! I'm through."

"Shut up," I said, stooping warily at his side. "We both know it'll take more than one measley bullet to kill that carcass."

"Went all the way through," he gasped. "Came out my damned back. Cat, it hurts like hell, it . . ."

Holstering the gun, I pulled his four hundred pounds to my shoulder and ran back across the open street to the comparative safety of another grounded shuttle. I tried to lay him gently on the grass, but every move was torture, as his pain-dulled grunts told me.

"Oh, my God," he mumbled.

"We can hold out here until Doc gets that door up," I whispered an attempt at encouragement.

He coughed up another flood of crimson fluid. "I'm drowning, Cat, don't let me drown!"

I pulled him to his side.

Shots from close by snapped my head around. Finnegan was laying down cover fire for the others as they dashed in all directions in diversionary desperation. You could read the terror on Horace's face when the little guy scuttled along the paving on all fours, and Holly clutched Linda so tightly to her breast that I felt sure she would smother the poor girl. Lew and Jeff were also firing their guns, though with less frequency and assuredness than Finnegan. Doc was still punching the panel.

Taking the hint, I pulled my stunner and began to fire blue pot shots into the darkness. Bull continued to struggle for breath at my side.

Slowly a tide of soldiers was advancing on us. In short sprints from one bit of cover to the next they came, firing high-powered rifles and sawed-off riot guns to keep us honest. A sand spray of pellets knicked me across the right forearm in several painful places, but I wasn't worried, as I knew they would heal within the hour. However, I did pull back to avoid any direct hits.

"I've got it!" screamed Doc Starett ecstatically. "It's open!"

My hungry eyes seized the view of the open ship door, and I let out an involuntary scream of my own. "He did it, Bull, he *did* it!" I spun around to grasp the big man by the shoulders. "We're getting off this—" The cold film of death was over his still face, the bubbles no longer bursting from his mouth.

The rain was suddenly hot on my face as I saw Gary Eisel and my beautiful Sheila. "Oh damn," I whispered, "damn, damn, damn, damn..."

The rest were now dodging for the inviting entrance ramp, and Chuck and Finnegan were the first to make it. Holly called out for me in confusion, and, standing as she was in the middle of the street, she was an open target for the advancing marksmen. Leaping to my feet, I caught her under one arm and ran for the ship.

Hadji and Ellen were, as always, together, but as they neared the craft, one Kurtz trooper zipped between them and their goal. Hadji twisted in front of the woman he loved, and the trooper fired his short, vicious riot gun.

The blast struck the man in the chest with the full fury of both barrels, and, as I watched from behind, he was lifted from the ground and forced back, with his feet rising in front of him. He hit on the pavement with his head and shoulders taking the full brunt of the fall and a sickening grinding sound in our ears. When he finally lay still, I could see the mangled ruin that had been his face.

The soldier, too, was dead before he could re-aim the gun at Ellen. She had leaped on him like a tigress a split second after Hadji hit the street, and the man's throat was torn out in a spring of gushing blood by her claws and teeth. He couldn't even cry out as he fell to the ground under her fury, and she, in an hysterical rage, continued to slash at his disintegrating face despite the fact that the bullets of his companions were singing off the street all about her.

From the ramp, we called out to her, but Ellen was so convulsively wild, crying and screaming at once, that she remained in the steaming remains of the murderer. Not sensible enough to talk myself out of it, I sprang across the intervening forty feet and grabbed her from behind.

She lashed out at me with a sweeping motion that would have left me blind for a week had I not ducked in time and caught her wrists in my right hand. She twisted like a snake, but was no match for me, and I clutched her as she collapsed in wracking sobs.

A shot rattled off the paving at our feet, and I was back on the ramp in another leap.

"Get her inside!" I shouted to Garner. "Is everybody here?"

"Horace!" shouted Linda from the interior. "He's not here!"

Jeff and I were the only ones on the ramp, and he saw the missing man before I did. "Over there!" he said, elbowing me and pointing at another shuttle at least fifty yards away. "Horace! Come on, we're ready!"

The other didn't reply, only huddling down further behind the shelter of the craft.

"What the hell is he doing?" I demanded.

"He's too afraid—no, wait, he's pulling...he's pulling Bull!"

"He's dead, Horace! Bull is *dead*!"

In a terrible moment of realization, Horace glanced wildly down at the corpse he had dragged so far across the wet street.

"Run for it!" Jeff yelled.

I drew the stunner and began to beam it out in a random pattern to keep the soldiers in position, and Jeff joined me with the handgun. He continued to spur Horace on with pleas and curses.

The monkey man was at home in the trees, but on the ground, especially paved ground, he was awkward and inefficient. Even with the fear of death pushing him on, Horace could only race toward us in a rolling welter of arms and legs that scrabbled like some huge spider in the street.

"Run!" Jeff was begging at the limit of his voice.

And I was screaming, too, unaware, and nearly everyone inside was shouting in a single voice for the little man to make it into the safety of our midst. But again that cold hand reached up from its place in the earth and touched us with its dispassionate mockery of our frailty. A burst of automatic gunfire erupted from behind our curtain of fire and chased Horace for a moment before knocking him ten feet as it smashed his hips.

He rolled over, panting, and began to crawl toward the ship.

I was blasting in one continuous electric steam then and hitting people, but not enough. Jeff was still calling hoarsely to him.

"Don't leave me, please," he cried in agony while he pulled his broken body to us. "Please!"

Another stream of fire raked Horace, shattering his throat and head.

"You goddamned sons of bitches!" Jeff threw down his gun and ran into the rain. He instinctively blended into his surroundings, but the downpour flowed over his solid form, making him resemble a glistening, silvery bubble. And a perfect target.

He caught a bullet before he was halfway to the lifeless body that was his goal. Leaping down, I caught him by the arm and dragged him back into the ship, thrusting aside those who clustered there.

"Close the door, Doc!" Chuck shouted to a point deeper in the ship. "Get to the couches so we can lift!"

"I certainly hope I can navigate this vehicle," said Doc as he hit the ignition switch.

When the roaring filled my ears and the great weight blanketed me, I squeezed Holly's small hand tighter, drawing as much strength from her as she from me. We had "made it."

9

"The Other Side of Light"

Doc launched us into supralight as soon as we were safely outside of Capella's system, only an hour later. The troops on Thear couldn't trail us in the unequipped shuttles, and the ponderous transfer boats could only make the trip in seven months or more. So, though they knew where we were undoubtedly headed, there was no way to warn Kurtz, for at least four months after we would have landed, anyway.

The leap into Tachyon Drive was much like the descriptions I had read in several pre-Plague fiction books. Strapped to our couches, we underwent a sudden feeling of acute nausea and internal disruption and then relief. Visual screens showed us nothing but unbroken black velvet, and only the lack of detectable gravity made us feel that we were truly in space.

After checking the computer's projected course set for Earth, Doc looked for and located a well-stocked medical cabin and cleaned and treated the wounded among us, the worst of whom was Jeff. This done, we ate an unsettling meal of concentrated protein and rested. I slept soundly.

Three months of seldom relieved boredom spiced with expectant yearnings is a long time. There were no "freezing down coffins" on this ship, since large parties rarely made trips on a communication vessel, but we did find thousands of microfilmed periodicals, films, and musical performances, as well as a fine variety of sports and games designed for weightless employment. There was one especially built lower room in which we passengers could undergo a period of simulated Earth weight by donning treated suits that would react with the adjustable electro-magnetic

111

floor. Doc, who virtually dictated on-board policy, made sure that each of us, himself included, spent an appreciable amount of time in there everyday; he also instituted an extensive medical program utilizing drugs that combatted the silent ravages of prolonged weightlessness.

Holly and I discovered that a common planetside enjoyment can take on new dimensions in weightless space, though it can also prove somewhat dangerous. Mass remains, even if weight vanishes.

The first big problem arose only four days out.

Jeff and I were floating a couple of feet over the floor in the darkened room, watching pre-Plague films flashed on the ceiling. I was personally trying to take things slowly, because I realized that boredom would be knocking at our door well before the ninety days were up.

Finnegan slid open the door and erased the old pictures with the light from the hallway. He glided into the room, in front of the projector, and presented us with a shadow picture that looked remarkably like a bunny with six ears.

"Do you mind?" I hinted to him.

"Take a flying leap," he said cordially.

Finnegan was prone to such expressive discourses and, because of this and other factors, really didn't have a single friend aboard the ship (not that it bothered him). Everyone—except possibly a fearless Thumper and a withdrawn Shana—allowed his insults and attempts at occasional fraternization simply because he had the ability and temperament to punch your teeth out if angered. We didn't bow and scrape to him, but for the sake of harmony, we didn't go out of our way to antagonize him, either.

"Passed Caribou in the hall," he spoke in a tone obviously meant for my ears.

I looked at Jeff. "Mark the date in your diary. That's something that doesn't happen once a day on this ship."

"Nope. Fifty times a day, maybe," Nichols said

"You know, she ain't bad looking, considering," Finnegan continued. "Good body, nice face, hair. Looks fine except for that repulsive skin."

"Shall I make an appointment for her with the staff dermatologist?" Jeff asked me.

Finnegan chuckled. "Yeah, and the way she's stuck on you, Cat, I'll bet you know just how good she is, don't you?"

I smiled sarcastically. "I know many things; I'm the Shadow."

"I think maybe I'll go find her and see for myself if she's as smooth as she looks."

Still smiling, I said, "You lay a hand on her and I'll break your face."

That startled him, but only a little. "Cat, I met you maybe a year ago, right? So how come I haven't killed you, yet?"

"Beats me. My glib wit and personal charm, perhaps?"

"I don't think it'll be too much longer 'til we get matters straight, me and you," he observed, floating slowly back into the hallway.

"Oh, please don't hurry on my account," I called after him.

Jeff sighed. "That fellow's got all the appeal of a meal that won't stay where it's put."

"Yeah, but I think he's slipping. There's not a broken bone on me."

We would have continued, but a feminine scream cut us off. It came from the next cabin.

"Caribou?" Jeff asked quickly.

"I don't think so."

"Bastard!" the girl's voice came again. "You raping, murdering bastard!" And we heard Finnegan laughing.

We swept into the hall. The next room was open, and the lights were on, so we got a good look at the situation that was developing within. Finnegan hovered in the near side of the cabin, a cruel grin twisting his features and his legs bunched against the wall ready to spring; Shana lay strapped lightly to a bunk in the other side and was holding one of the three pistols we had aboard, aiming it at Finnegan. There was no joy in her eyes, but I did see a hot need there, a vengeful need.

"You stinking, conceited son of a bitch," she hissed at him. "You really think you can come in any time and use a girl like some private possession, don't you? Like-like property! Well, I'm going to shoot that smile right off of your face, you scum!"

"I'll give you one shot, little sister," Finnegan answered her, "then I come on and tear that sweet little arm off at the shoulder."

"Hey, whoa!" I yelled. "Time out, you two. There's no reason for this—"

Shana swung the gun to cover me. "I'll get you next, Mr. Smug Male!"

My voice was little more than a tense whisper, "He'll do it, Shana, he'll *kill* you."

"Then he'll have to be faster than this bullet," she assured me.

"All of you freaks know only one kind of law, so I'll be glad to make peace myself."

Jeff tried his hand, "You know that Cat and Finnegan are fast enough to stop you, Shana, so why don't you let this drop before it goes too far and somebody gets hurt? I'm the only one you have a firm chance of plugging with that thing, and I haven't done anything to you, have I?"

The gun, which she held out before her in both hands, began to tremble. Her tone was pained and confused. "Leave me alone, Jeff, please leave me alone."

"I can't abandon you," he answered quietly. "If I go now and you use the gun, you'll be dead—"

"I *am* dead!" she screamed.

"No, you're not! You're almost home! If it doesn't work for us, it's our own skin, but with your friends, you *can* go back again. Don't throw it all away now."

And the pistol began to move. Slowly, tentatively, she began to draw it to herself and point the barrel away from us, her head shaking sadly. Just as evenly cautious, Jeff drifted past me into the room, across it, and lightly bumped the bed. "Can I have it?" he asked.

She nodded, and her weightless hair blossomed in a soft cloud about her head. "Take it," she replied.

Jeff did so, gingerly.

A flesh-colored bolt of lightning burst from the wall straight at Shana and Jeff. Instinctively, I pushed off from the doorway to intercept this sudden threat and, no more than five feet from the startled pair, Finnegan and I collided with a force that sent us both spinning like tops to finally slam viciously into the cabin wall.

"Open the door!" I yelled at Jeff while groping for a hold on the stunned, but dangerous Irishman.

He clutched at my throat with a tearing grip, but I wiggled free and caught myself against the solidness of the bunk. "Open the damned door!" I repeated before noticing that Jeff and already done so. Then, anchoring myself by the bed frame, I kicked at Finnegan's struggling body with both feet and hit him in the center of the back.

If the door had been six inches narrower, he wouldn't have made it, but, as it was, he sailed out only to smash into the steel side of the hallway and renew his varied and loud cursing. Jeff palmed the door shut and leaned against it.

"Phew," he sighed, "two points for you, Cat, and I don't want to play anymore."

Jerking a thumb at the hall, I gasped, "Sure, but I don't think *he* will let us retire undefeated."

Jeff literally bounced from the door as Finnegan slammed into the other side, bellowing profanity and abundant promises of all sorts of imaginative mayhem centered upon the three of us. Shana reached for the gun, but I was close enough to snatch it away and push the button on the room's call box.

"Chuck Garner," I said on the open circuit, "paging Mr. Garner, oh, Chuck, hey, Chuck!"

I let up on the button and waited. Presently, his voice answered, "Garner here. What's the problem?"

Jeff rolled his eyes and intoned in a mystified aborigine dialect, "Magic box talk like man! Great Spirit live in box, much juju!"

I laughed and I answered Chuck's question, "Cat here, Chuck; Jeff, Shana, and I are in room seven, and, contrary to popular belief, we are *not* having a depraved, morally reprehensible display of the depths to which three humans can sink. That's not because we aren't trying—"

"Why, then?" asked the magic box.

As if on cue, Finnegan hit the door again, actually leaving it dented under a pounding it was never meant to take.

"I don't know if you heard that or not," I said, "but there's this unsatisfied customer out in the hall who just may try a few revolutionary meatloaf recipes with our brains unless you get somebody down here, pronto, as we say in Sheboygan."

"Don't tell me it's Finnegan again," he moaned.

"Then it'll be a mighty quiet conversation."

"What's the matter this time?"

"Let's just say he returned to the scene of the crime and let it go at that, okay? Now, about preserving my existence as a breathing member of this crew—"

"All right, just a minute. I think Doc has got a knockout shot he can fire from about fifty feet."

"Advise him to start practicing, and *hurry*, damn it!"

The communications ship had a very well-equipped brig, for situations that might arise when transporting mutant captives during the rare trip back to Earth and taking care of their own men, should the just thoughts of Director Kurtz somehow desert their heads. After Starett tranquilizing Finnegan as he would any other rampaging animal—from a distance and in concealment—Chuck

115

heard our testimony and decided the immediate fate of the wild Irishman. Where he had once been a huge potential asset to our band, he had developed into a moody, unpredictable, and very dangerous liability aboard the inflight ship.

"Take him to the brig," Garner finally ordered, "and put him in deep alpha sleep for the rest of the flight. Doc, you're in charge of his well-being."

And the problem was solved, temporarily.

My lapses into the unidentifiable daydreams were still frequent on the trip, just as they had become after the teen-aged executioner invaded my mind back in New Casper. They weren't flashes of unconsciousness or imaginary screenplays. They were tenuous, fragile glimpses of a past that I had never experienced.

On our second month out, I spoke of them to others for the first time. Things had quietened down a good bit. Finnegan was still snoozing peacefully; Ellen had begun to accept, if not understand, the death of her lover for five years; and Shana had opened her shell just a crack, speaking and occasionally smiling. She had even half-allowed my infrequent advances, and I'm sure Jeff did better than I.

Only Mike still had problems. The months-old wound on his back had not healed and nightmares, screaming, battling nightmares were now the rule during the short periods that the big fellow slept. He was badly worried, and so was Doc, secretly.

Starett, Holly, and I were eating (that is, squeezing balanced nutritional meals into our mouths from plastic packets) when I had the tall, tall building lapse. One of the others was talking, but I was sitting crosslegged on a dirty sidewalk in the middle of the New York City of a hundred years ago.

"You sick, man?" a passerby in the vision asked me.

"Nah," I said, shaking my head and craning my neck to stare up at the unbelievable height of one of the towering buildings. *"Just scared."*

"Eli!" came an insistent whisper from outside the dream. It was followed by a soft punch on my shoulder.

"Yeah?" I replied, clearing my head.

"Doc was talking to you!"

"Sorry, old man, what did you say?"

He grinned quizzically at me before answering, "May I ask where you were a moment ago?"

"Of course you may."

"Okay then, where?"

"New York."

"Well, that explains your attitude of insular preoccupation. It's probably difficult to understand my words in New York, which is roughly twenty-two light years away."

"You said it."

"Seriously, though, haven't I noticed these 'daydreams' of yours quite often?"

"I suppose so; they have gotten stronger and more frequent since that foul-up back in New Casper."

"What daydreams?" Holly had braided her long hair into two strands that weren't so unmanageable in the weightlessness, and the effect was one of girlishness.

So I explained my lifelong acquaintance with occasional, extremely retainable glimpses of experiences that I had never undergone and how, sometimes, these dreams came during sleep and were then longer and even more vivid. To top these confessions, I hit them with my rather unconventional account of the festivities in New Casper. "And," I summed up, "the script now calls for the both of you to guffaw rudely and give highly descriptive comments concerning my veracity, character, and immediate heritage."

Doc almost took me up on it. "Your record of your 'visions' is coherent and believable, but that section about the New Casper executioner... come now, Cat."

Holly believed, but she always was gullible. "Do you mean that girl's mind was transferred?"

I nodded.

Doc snorted out a chuckle. "Brain transplantation is a distinct possibility, but personalities surely can't be transposed without *any* physical conduction."

"That sounds reasonable."

"Yet you persist in this obviously fanciful belief?"

I sighed heavily, somewhat intimidated by his high-priced terminology. "Listen, Doc, all I know is that I saw an unarmed boy kill a man with his mind and then come into my own skull for the same purpose. Somehow I made it backfire on him. So, *you* explain it to *me*."

Maybe my sincerity impressed him. Thoughtfully adjusting his glasses, he nodded a little. "Perhaps... perhaps I have been hasty in my skepticism. Up until my capture by the authorities, I hadn't come across any qualified studies concerning the aspects of *mental* mutations. It's possible that this 'executioner' has evolved the ability to subjugate the brains of others and will their deaths, as it

117

were. Though it still seems outlandish, I can't factually deny his power to transfer the...the *essence*, the *soul*, if you will, of a human and relocate it in the physical confines of some other creature."

Holly was staring at me, somewhat fearfully. "Then, does that mean that Eli might...?"

How unknowingly prophetic!

"The evidence suggests that he has some hidden—and considerable, I'd say—power in this same area."

That was both frightening and interesting. "So how come I haven't zapped some of my too numerous to mention enemies into zombieland already?"

"Who can say at this point? Personally, I would guess that it is a reservoir so crude and deeply buried in your psyche that it can only be exicted by another direct assault of mental force."

"This is a lot to take in at once, you know?"

"Undoubtedly. Why don't we take up the subject, explore it more thoroughly, in another session? *Sine die*?"

I was in agreement, but, for a number of reasons, that next meeting never came.

Like the previous two, the third month had its standout occurrence. Unfortunately, this one was far more tragic than the others.

In the artificially heated, weightless interior of an interstellar vessel, there were actually no reasons for conventional beds and blankets, other than the psychological ones, but the designers felt that these latter reasons were enough to provide five rooms with four bunks apiece. A soft, flexible sheet was included on each to comfortably anchor the inhabitant(s) to the frame by electromagnetic linings.

Shana, Linda, and Ellen (and sometimes Jeff) regularly slept in room seven; Mike, Lew, and Chuck sacked out in varied schedules in room eight; and Finnegan, of course, was still having his long snooze in the brig. Doc usually caught his winks in a couch before the main control panel of the ship, though he occasionally got lucky with one of the girls or spent time alone in room nine. No one actually knew where or when Thumper slept, only that it wasn't in a bed. Holly and I occupied room ten, and number eleven was a sort of spare. In case of guests.

The two of us were alone in ten that "night" and were sleeping soundly under the magnetic blanket, with no hint of the approaching danger. The sliding doors operated with only a ghostly hiss, but that was enough to sting my alert ears and awaken me with the speed that life on Thear had bred. In the soft light from the hall, I recognized the huge, hulking figure of Mike Bolger.

"Oh, hi, Mike," I yawned sleepily at him. "S'matter? Back giving you problems?"

He didn't answer, sliding quietly toward us. Holly slept on.

"Maybe Doc can give you something," I rambled on while he came. "Man, I just wish Joanna had come along with some of her herbs and—"

And he hit me. With the driving force of his six hundred pounds, his knotted right fist smashed into my face, and only instinctive rolling with the punch saved a shattered jaw and cheekbone. Another bolt of lightning licked across my ribs as I bounced into the mattress next to Holly.

"God... Mike," I gasped, trying to catch his flailing fists, "what's the matter?"

"You damned demon," he was crying. "You did it, you did it!"

"What? It's me, Mike, Cat—" I was punched quiet by another direct hit in the face. An insulated cloud wrapped about my head, as he slammed again and again.

Consciousness slipped in and out of my grasp for the next several minutes, until, apparently satisfied with my state of battering, he ripped me from the bed and tossed me aside. Floating painfully against the ceiling, I fuzzily saw the giant grasp a screaming Holly by her braids and drag her nude from the bed.

"You laughed, didn't you?" he was still crying. Then he hit her, hard, in the stomach and drove the breath from her. She was choking for air when he hit her again, and she spewed vomit in a wet, brown eruption.

Enough awareness returned for me to kick off from the roof and strike back. I tried to pin his massive arms and not use my fists, because it was obvious that he was totally irrational. He was a strong brute and fought me like an animal, but I managed to free Holly and wrestle him through the doorway, shouting the entire time for help. Thumper came sailing out of somewhere.

"He's crazy!" I yelled over Mike's grunts and curses. "Help me hold him!"

Thumper grabbed his right arm and I the left, but that was a big mistake. Unanchored and weightless, we were like decorations on Bolger's arms, and he waved us savagely. I whumped into a wall at a speed highly dangerous to my health.

One arm freed, Mike began to swipe at Thumper, who, in turn, roared and started for the other's head with obvious intentions. "Don't kill him, Thumper!" I shouted. "He can't help it!"

The ape man pulled up, and Mike had the advantage he needed to shoot down the hall. He bowled past a startled Doc into the control room.

We covered him there, all of us, and tried our damnedest to stop his rampage without hurting him, but in his blind, screaming rage, he wouldn't be stopped. He beat us away, broke free of our grasps, tore bolted couches from the floor, and smashed the glowing circuits on the panels. Doc tried to drug him with the hypo gun that had been used on Finnegan, but he put Starett and the gun out of action by clubbing him down with a section of metal pipe.

Thumper and I were relied upon to restrain him by using our strength, and either of us should have been equal to the task had we been in a no-holds-barred war. However, restricted by our concern, we couldn't match his wild ferocity.

Finally Bolger stood glaring at us, his back against the main panel and one hand raised menacingly above it. He struck down once, and sparks flew in spectacular firefalls.

"If he destroys the panel, we'll be kicked out of supralight drive and lose control of the ship!" Doc yelled.

Mike smashed the pipe into the arcing mess.

"Stop him," Chuck whispered. "Do it, Thumper."

A ball of hair and muscle hit Bolger just as he raised the pipe for the last time. Mike screamed only once before his thick, muscular neck snapped under the awesome pressure of Thumper's arms.

"Jesus," said Chuck, "oh, Jesus . . ."

Doc, whose own arm was broken, checked our wounds and did what he could to ease the pain. One of his prime concerns was that none of us had been bitten or clawed by our dead companion. Mike's convulsion had, he theorized, resulted from a malevolent infection incurred on Thear during his encounter with the leech-creatures, and could probably be passed into a new host through his saliva.

"Like a rabid dog," Holly commented.

I watched Chuck pull the lifeless body out of the cabin to a storage room below. We couldn't eject him in Tachyon Drive.

"And what do we do with rabid dogs?" I muttered to myself in anger and sorrow.

"We kill them," Jeff replied, "even if they're human and have saved our necks a hundred times."

Now, we were only eleven.

10

"Planetfall"

It was a dream "long time coming," something you hoped for fervently, but never really expected to live to see. It was Earth.

For five long months, we had struggled from the depths with this one goal; we had fought, killed, and seen our number reduced one by one, often needlessly, and only this ultimate destination sustained our lagging spirits. Shana had been away the shortest span of time, about ten months, including the voyage to Thear, and Holly, Jeff, and myself had been away from our homes approximately eighteen months. At the other end of the spectrum, Ellen, the loss of Hadji still painful in her mind, could hardly conceive a return to her home planet. She had been deported over twelve years before, half of her lifetime.

So, eighty-seven days after blast off, Doc informed us that we would slip below light in the next two hours, and the excitement darted like electricity throughout the ship. Everyone had plans.

"After I personally smear Director Kurtz' disgusting profile over all of the available landscape," Jeff proclaimed, "I shall then proceed to spend the next consecutive ninety hours in blissful slumber."

Chuck, who was in the control room with the rest of us, shook his head in exaggerated disbelief. "I hope you don't plan this little exhibition for too soon," he said.

"Why not?"

"To begin with, we can't just set this tub down in Kurtz' lap—"

"Sounds like an excellent site for the retrorockets to me."

"...*because* his personal W. H. O. flunkies would blow our heads off. We have to land as secretly as possible and then smuggle

Shana into the hands of her more influential friends, those who will be sympathetic to her plight. After that, we'll probably have to hide out until the news of Kurtz' coldblooded betrayal of an elected official causes his own political downfall."

"Hell, that could take months!"

"Could and most certainly will, Mr. Nichols, but any other action would be clear suicide."

"Why don't we just kidnap the old boy himself and show him the cold, hard facts?" I asked.

"Aside from the certainty that we could never get near him, we wouldn't be accepted as anything but mad renegades by the rest of Earth."

"Another year of this," I sighed.

"So what are you worried about?" Jeff pointed out. "You've kept up with your shaving; with some new caps in your mouth and forged papers, you shouldn't have any trouble passing."

"Sure, you, too," I answered. We looked meaningfully at Chuck and Holly, whose deformities were a bit more obvious. "Of course, that doesn't apply to everyone."

"I don't believe I've met these two blighters, old shoe," Jeff said thoughtfully. "You?"

"Never laid eyes nor ears on 'em," I replied. "It's *so* nice to be normal."

"Elias Blaine Harper, if you ever try to pull something like that on me, I'll squeal to the police so loudly, they'll shoot you on sight!" threatened Holly.

"You know, I believe she would."

Scheduled flights from Thear usually dropped out of Tachyon Drive about three and a half billion miles from the Sun, near the orbit of Pluto, giving them some decelerating and maneuvering time before approaching Earth. (The predicted months of deceleration following faster than light speeds had not proven to be needed.) However, because this early slowing allowed outer Earth stations to track and anticipate arrivals, Doc planned to pull off a dangerous technique for one so inexperienced in piloting. Relying heavily on the ship's computers, he proposed that we delay deceleration until about a sixth as far away, placing us just outside Jupiter and allowing us the advantage of surprise. With some tricky calculating on the part of man and machine, he could touch us down in some isolated area inside of an hour following deceleration. It would be a very ticklish undertaking.

At Doc's recommendation, we strapped ourselves into the

couches, and Lew commented, "For once, I wish I were Catholic and had a Saint Christopher medal to fondle."

"You have to have faith in our navigator," I told him.

Doc calmly chilled the blood in my veins by saying, "Faith would hardly play a significant part in these proceedings, Cat. A large variety of things could go wrong easily enough. Our shields could fail and allow us to be mortally damaged by a piece of space material; I could be too slow in my personal reactions and send us into a fiery end on Earth; the computer may have malfunctioned and hurled us along in the wrong direction; armed ships could be—"

"You've made your point," I admitted.

And, with considerable fear and trembling, we began to slow. At a point still known as the speed of light, that previously experienced nausea and interior twisting gripped each of us, and we were once again in normal, if tremendous, speed.

"Did we make it, Doc?" Chuck asked excitedly.

"Just a . . . minute, I have to check my readings . . . um, yes, yes, we seem to be within six thousand miles of our projected arrival point." Starett's voice was as cool and emotionless as the machine he was handling.

But a cheer of sorts broke from our queasy throats. We were back in our own solar system, far closer to Earth than most of us had ever expected to be again, and we could feel the solidness of home beneath our feet.

"You did it, you test tube tinker!" congratulated Jeff, eagerly unstrapping himself.

We clustered about his couch, as he obliviously continued his swift adjustments with the ship that still had to get us back to the blue planet. At speeds that were yet incomprehensible, we flashed sunward, slowing and adjusting all the while. I'll swear that it was no more than an hour before the main view screen presented a dot of light that became two, then a globe and its satellite, and, finally, Earth and the Moon.

"This is beautiful," Holly said for all of us.

"Where?" Doc asked Chuck.

"Can you get us in upstate New York? Outside Albany, maybe?"

"Easily enough. We'll be detected, of course, but there are no W. H. O. military complexes within five hundred miles other than the administrative board in New York City. Also, I can bring it in under local radar coverage. We should be able to land the vehicle and relaunch it on a decoy flight before our position can be pinpointed."

"You do that, Doc," said Chuck, "and I'll kiss you!"

"Uh, could you delegate that task to Ellen, or Caribou, or Linda?"

"Damned right!" Garner laughed.

"Good. Well, back to your couches. Touchdown in thirteen minutes."

It was too close, too good to be real. Nevertheless, that blue and green ball continued to grow on the screen as we sailed into the third, and hopefully final phase of our plan.

Either the autopilot or Doc's skill was in top form that day, as the craft burned its way through the layers of atmosphere to bump lightly against the ground. Our elation came first, but it was quickly accompanied by a smothering, pressing feeling of heaviness that drove us deeply into the cushioning. Gravity had returned after a long hiatus.

"I'm glad I spent plenty of time in the weight room," I puffed, trying to unstrap myself. "It kept my muscles in fine fettle."

Jeff laughed loudly between gasps. "If everyone were in the shape you are, there'd be one heckava lot more twenty-year-old heart attacks victims."

"Jealous," I grunted, sitting on the edge of the couch.

Thumper jerked off his straps and swung to the floor as lightly as he had moved back on Thear. The rest of us looked on enviously.

"Okay, you guys," Chuck called out, "you can stop your groaning and move it. We need to reset this thing and blast it off in the next ten minutes, and I haven't heard anyone volunteering for a return voyage."

The readjustment to weight hurt, but, like our first journey to Thear, we had undergone constant inflight chemotherapy and electrolytic stimulation, and our actual physical condition was good.

After a few minutes of strains, grumbles, and dizziness, we were basically ready to depart. Doc, his lower right arm almost wholly healed thanks to modern medicine, remained at the control panel and hurriedly punched in a new automatic course, which the computer verified and accepted.

"You done yet?" Chuck asked.

"Almost," he muttered. "After she blasts, she'll head out fifteen degrees east of the big meridian. From there, if the patrols don't blow her out of the sky, she'll hit Tachyon Drive just outside of the moon's orbit and head for Regulus. Let them try to follow her *there*!"

"All right, but hurry. They'll be looking for us already."

124

"What about Finnegan?" I said. I saw a fleeting light in Shana's eyes.

Chuck paused. "We can't leave him on the ship, can we? And he sure as hell won't feel kindly toward us when we wake him. Cat, you and Thumper go down, unhook him, tie him up, if you can find something strong enough to hold him, and bring him along. We'll decide further after we get away from here."

"Why do I always get the garbage detail?"

We started to leave, but met Lew Chang coming up the ramp. He stopped us. "Don't bother, boys, the Irishman's gone."

"Gone?"

"That's right. Straps and tubes were torn off, and the entire lower level is empty. Apparently, he was jarred awake when we dropped out of Tachyon and he skipped out an emergency hatch while we were moaning around up here."

Chuck had heard it all, and he answered with, "Damn, we can't worry about that now. Let's go. Are you ready, Doc?"

"All systems go."

"Everybody into the woods. Get at least a half mile away so we'll be out of range when the ship blasts. It's all forest around here, and we won't worry about being seen, yet."

We realized that we had landed on Earth near Albany, in the woods, and at night; what we hadn't considered was the season. Wearing only our W. H. O. issue and the pieces of the four uniforms we had stolen on Thear, we marched unprepared into the middle of a snow-blanketed December.

"Oh no," Holly said, as she stumbled down the ramp. Her words formed puffs in the night air, and she wore neither shoes or sleeves. "We'll freeze into icicles!"

"What's the matter?" I joked through already chattering teeth. "Nothing in the world like a little b-brisk night air to clear the mind."

"Well, I'm not going out in that," she declared.

"You will or spend the next six months on your way to Regulus," Garner told her.

"And I'm sure you wouldn't like the neighborhood," I added.

"Okay," Jeff complied simply. "I'm agreeable, anyhow."

Holly came, too.

We continued down the ramp onto the ground. This part wasn't too bad, since our landing jets had steamed away the snow covering for some forty feet around, and the ground was still warm. But we couldn't linger, as Chuck prodded us on with dire predictions should we get caught in the lifting blast. I already knew what the blast from a smaller craft could do.

Strangely enough, I was in the lead when we slogged through the wet clearing into the snowy surrounding forest. I gingerly stuck my bare right foot (Shana was wearing what was left of my trooper uniform, including the well-stuffed boots) into the freezing white cloak. A shock danced up my leg.

"Jeeze, Chuck," I gasped.

"Go on, Cat, we're following along."

"Oh, gee, that's so comforting."

A variety of shouts, squeals, and curses accompanied our progress, and, believe me, dressed only in trunks, I was blue in a matter of minutes. "We've got to get out of this, Chuck, or ten frozen bodies will be all that's left."

"Let's just concentrate on surviving right now," he stuttered back.

Jeff shouldered next to me, draping an arm around Holly's shivering shoulders in the process. "Where do you suppose Finnegan's disappeared to? I haven't seen the first track."

"Probably set off in the other direction to throw us off. Or maybe he's still hiding on the ship, which is fine with me since his opinion of myself was less than ecstatically admirable. Let him cool his heels around Regulus for a couple of thousand years." And that was heartfelt.

"Eli, you can't really mean that. It's inhuman to hope that he'll be sent so far away alone," objected Holly.

"Well, I *do* have a conscience, but, luckily, my cowardice continually overcomes it."

"This should be far enough," said Chuck. "Get down behind a tree or something and watch out for the flash. How long, Doc?"

"No more than ninety seconds."

I located the dark shape of a large tree and dug the snow from the away side of its trunk. The contact sent pain through my fingers, and I had to press them tightly under my arms to relieve the discomfort. I was shivering badly by then.

"W-want some c-company?" asked Holly, while I eased my posterior onto the hard ground.

"Sure. More the merrier. Misery loves it. A penny saved is a penny earned."

"H-huh?" Her teeth were chattering audibly.

"Bad joke."

She sat trembling next to me, and we snuggled, sharing each other's warmth.

"You've got to stop m-meeting this way," Jeff couldn't resist cracking from his own dug-out in the snow.

"Shield your eyes," Doc said quietly.

With characteristic good sense, I stuck my head around the tree and squinted in the direction we had travelled from. Starett was on the nose again, for, almost as soon as I looked, a flare-bright burst of light popped from a half mile back and was quickly followed by a dull rumble. The white glare climbed swiftly into the black sky and flashed into the distance.

"Let's hope she draws the dogs off our trail," Lew said.

"Let's hope for an unseasonable heat wave," Jeff countered.

Almost frighteningly, a brief cloud of blast-heated air rolled over us, just as, in the early days of liquid propellant space flight, these waves would travel as much as five miles before dispersing.

"Meet an ex-agnostic," puffed Nichols reverently.

But the delicious warmth was all too short, and Chuck had us moving again before we congealed where we sat. Holly soon began stumbling consistently, not from fatigue, but something far worse. I caught her once as she pitched forward, and she whispered, "I'm scared, Eli, I-I can't feel my feet!"

Stopping, I bent down to touch them, and incurred the disfavor of our leader to the rear. "What's the holdup, Cat? We don't have time for theatrics and bum wisecracks."

"Shove it," I advised him. "Holly can't go any further; she's dead from the ankles down." Her toes felt like small, cold stones in my palm. "We've got to start a fire or something."

"Not likely," Doc commented, "considering the condition of—"

"Then what the hell *can* we do?"

"Yeah, I'm not any better off," Lew admitted.

"Same here," added Ellen. "They just stopped hurting."

Shaking in the moonlight, Chuck disagreed, "We couldn't risk it, even if we could start one."

"Perhaps I have a portion of the solution," Starett said. "In a medical pouch I rescued from the ship, I believe we shall find . . . one, two . . . um, five stimulants in capsule form. They'll accelerate the metabolic rate, increase heat production, and give each user a certain amount of protection from serious frostbite for up to three hours."

"A-Adjustinin," said Jeff, using the brand name, "bad medicine. Make you . . . woosh . . . makes you start digesting your insides."

I lifted Holly from the snow. "It's all we've got. Break 'em out."

Chuck took over the lead, "With only five, we'll have to consider the distribution—"

"How's this?" Jeff broke in. "You've got clothes and shoes, so has Shana. The other two sets are on Mike's body, headed for God knows where, and-and on Finnegan's back, and *he's* probably l-laughing at us right now. That leaves eight of us as prime con-contenders."

Linda, who had been riding fairly warm in one of Shana's pockets, popped her head up and said, "Count me out."

Thumper sat in the snow, apparently oblivious to the temperature. He mumbled, "Don't need any."

"You sure?" Jeff asked.

Thumper stared silently in answer.

"Hokay. T-that leaves . . . uh, six, right?"

"Five," I said. "I come from a cold climate."

"No," Chuck stopped me, "we still need you, Cat. And Jeff, Doc, Ellen, Lew."

"And Holly," I finished. "She can have mine."

"Don't get melodramatic," Garner said.

"Melodramatic, hell! Her feet are frozen!"

"So carry her. If yours freeze, we'll have two liabilities, and this thing is far from over. Don't pull any of these phony self-sacrificing routines."

"Enough of this!" Doc said abruptly. "Albany should be within a couple of hours of here, and it's ridiculous to stand here quibbling." He handed the capsules to Jeff, Lew, Ellen, and myself.

"Take it," Holly whispered.

So I did.

The pill worked with amazing speed. Even as the others commented on similar reactions, I felt a liquid warmth spreading from high in my stomach, as if I had drunk of hot coffee, and it travelled throughout my body until even my sharply paining toes were blessed with the internal heat. "This is terrific!" I said.

"But limited in duration," replied Doc.

"Which way?" Chuck asked him.

"Due north. We should be able to find a shelter in the city."

Jeff, feeling better already, spoke up, "Which side of the moss do the trees grow on?"

"This way," I said, carrying Holly in the direction I knew instinctively to be north. They followed.

Holly curled up tightly in my arms and warmed her feet with her hands. As the Adjustinin continued to work, even she felt it, saying, "Your skin feels so *hot*." I laughed giddily, not realizing that the drug would also produce a "stoned" reaction in the user.

We soon came across a deserted highway that led to Albany.

In 1980, Albany, New York had been a city of almost one hundred and twenty thousand resident souls. In 1990, it held close to three and a half million. That December, 2029, thirty-one years after the Plague, the city of Albany could boast a population of only five thousand two hundred and seventy-nine. At approximately two-thirty p.m., ten fugitives from Earth B marched into the sparsely settled city, five a little less steadily than the others, because they were bombed.

"Wake up, you bilious buzzards!" Jeff shouted to the empty streets. The inhabitants were all sleeping warmly in their apartments, and row upon row of padlocked, unused stores, hotels, and office buildings waited for the owners that had failed to come for thirty years. Albany had been hit hard.

"Will you shut up?" Chuck whispered from behind.

"Yeah," I laughed too loudly, "you talk off-key."

"Good Lord," sighed Garner. "I've got five winos on my hands."

"Let's sing Christmas carols!" suggested Ellen, as she and Lew stumbled along supporting one another. "The last Christmas I ever had was in . . . in 2017. I was just a little girl—" Suddenly, she was crying.

"Hey, don't do that," I said, choking up myself. "Listen, let's sing the carols, like . . . uh, 'There was a young woman named Mabel, who lived all her life in a stable; the colts that lived there, thought she was a mare, who was ready, willing and able.'" I broke into a sustained peal of laughter along with my four cohorts. Jeff even fell to the street and lay in helpless mirth.

"I heard one of those," gasped Doc between chuckles. "It had something to do with a fellow named Cass and 'Stormy Weather' and . . ."

"I can see this is going to go on for hours," Chuck said resignedly, "so we've got to get them to sleep somewhere out of sight. What about it, Shana?"

"I don't know where we could go. We had a house here, but I'm sure that Dad sold it sometime last summer, or the summer before we left, I mean," she replied.

"What about clothes? We've got to hide these tattoos, if nothing else."

"There are several clothing shops still in business. Welles', that big store on the corner just down the street, carries clothes, shoes, almost everything, but how could we get in?"

"Break in," Garner said.

"Discreetly, of course," I added.

"No, we can't do that. All of the doors and windows are wired with alarms," she said.

"Who said anything about doors and windows?" I asked Holly, who I still carried because it was yet only fifteen or twenty degrees above zero. "Did you?"

"Um um," she breathed coldly.

Chuck was tired, and his voice reflected it. "Cat, please shut up until you sober up, okay?"

"Good question. I'll have to think about it someday." Thus, quietly, I marched away from them into an alley next to the large store that Shana had promised would contain everything we needed or wanted. Like a for real hamburger, for instance. The building was old and sided with weathered brown brick.

I sat Holly delicately on an ashcan, which didn't do her any good at all, and then stared blearily at the aged wall. It stared infuriatingly back. "All right, you s.o.b.," I slurred, "be that way."

"Eli, what are you—"

I punched the wall.

Bits of shattered brick flew, and my right arm accordioned behind the fist. If I had been sober, the pain would have elicited a profoundly soulful scream from my lips. It didn't break any bones, but the skin was torn from my knuckles and a small depression was left in the bricks. A straight left knocked a full brick from the wall and smashed two others to rubble. I now had a slight, but definite hole to work with.

"What in the world are you doing?" Holly blurted out.

"By-passing, my dear," I answered, pulling out large chunks of ancient brick with my bleeding hands. "Simply by-passing."

Considering the fact that the Adjustinin was wearing off and leaving me with a used-up, dizzy feeling, I tore a man-sized opening in the outer brick, dug through the fiberglas insulation, and punched in the interior panelling with a fair amount of speed. While the others still shuffled around in front of the building, trying to decide a plan of attack, Holly and I stumbled into the darkness of the same.

"No wiring in the walls," Doc muttered to himself later over a steaming cup of black coffee, his first in three years. "I certainly should have thought of that."

"I wish I hadn't," I said, massaging my wounded knuckles.

Once inside the store, we had located the main power box, turned up the heating system, switched on a few unobtrusive lights, and fixed ourselves a much-needed hot meal in the cafeteria. Over a hamburger and hot chocolate (I don't smoke, either), I tried to ease a throbbing head.

Chuck sat in a booth with his micro-broiled steak and pondered our next move. Due to our unorthodox method of entry, our little stopover in Welles' would most probably be discovered early the next morning, and, since Shana knew of no valuable contacts in Albany, it would certainly be to our advantage to be long gone by daybreak. We needed clothes to disguise ourselves, money, and some form of papers to allow us freedom of travel on the railway system. Meanwhile, we ate.

"Got a good little cook there, Colonel," Jeff said while dipping another golden french fry in a glob of ketchup. Holly sat next to us on the barstools and smiled.

"Passable," I replied. "How are the feet, honey?"

"They hurt," she admitted, "but that's good because they're not numb anymore. You kept me so warm that they didn't get frostbitten, I guess."

"Let's hurry up, people. It'll be four o'clock in a few minutes, and Shana tells me that a train passes through at five," Chuck said to us.

"You mean a regular passenger train makes a daily stop in this place?" Ellen asked.

"The schedule runs through here from the upper states," Garner explained. "If there are any passengers in the station, they'll stop."

I had never been much of a clotheshorse, so I quickly selected a conservative dark suit, shoes, wallet, and raincoat. It would have been out of style even before I was deported to Thear, but I had no desire to call attention to myself.

The range of outfits made it obvious to us that the "classical costume" was in vogue in the current fashion world, and Jeff went all out with a Three Musketeers uniform that included huge boots, an extravagant velvet cape, a full-brimmed, plumed hat, and a dress sword. He bandished the prop theatrically and was heard to shout, "Be warned, ye varlets and scalawags, the Avenging Blade is abroad once more," on more than one occasion.

Holly, because she had so much more to conceal than the rest of us, chose a long blue gown with matching gloves and a small hat with a veil that allowed her lengthy hair to flow from beneath it but hid the unfortunate aspects of her face. She obviously enjoyed primping before the full-length mirrors and adjusting now unfamiliar undergarments to her best advantage. The sight did me some good, also, as I washed my hands in a warm, soupy solution to aid their scabbing.

Ellen dressed similarly, the gloves covering her nails and the dress her tail; Shana simply picked an outfit she felt most flattering to her; and Linda sat by watching disconsolately. Doc hid his extra arms under a heavy overcoat, just as he had in pre-discovery days, while Lew followed my example in dull vestments. Thumper and Chuck presented problems, and we partially solved the first by dressing the ape man in children's clothing, trimming his hair, and shaving him. His arms still protruded at least a foot beyond his cuffs but an adult's half-coat helped here. Chuck's problem was just as difficult, and a fur-collared overcoat with a low, wide-brimmed hat were the best we could do. His ears were covered, but his nose would occasionally poke out of the shadows.

Ready cash was provided by the instore currency which Thumper obligingly secured for us by smashing into an office safe with a crowbar. Our papers were drawn up by Doc in a very private printing room in the basement of the building (after he had located some uncracked eyeglasses that closely matched his own in the optical department). We all had to have new names, and I was suddenly Augustus Baldwin, twenty-seven, of Vero Beach, Florida. It wasn't likely that anyone would bother to check with Vero Beach.

Thus, it was with reluctance that we left the warmth of Welles Department Store for the wintry night of Albany and its single operating train depot. We were a strange-looking crew of nine (hidden in one of Ellen's pockets, Linda didn't count), and the only other person in the depot was an old, bored ticket man who eyed us with a certain amount of suspicion. Somehow, I managed to be shoved to the lead of the line before his window.

"Ayh?" he grunted at me.

I flashed my forged papers officially. "Augustus Baldwin. Vero Beach."

"So?"

"I need a ticket on the train."

"Where to?"

"Uh . . ." I twisted around, looking for prompting from Chuck.

"New York, you fool," he whispered.

"Yeah, New York City."

His suspicions were not allayed in the least when the eight people behind me purchased tickets for the same destination (especially not when Thumper grunted "N'Yok" in an adult bass and had to be called back for his change), but he remained sullenly quiet until the train slid into a long stop on its single rail. Then we boarded easily enough and were soon seated in reclining chairs with our suitcases of stolen clothing at our feet. Though the trip would be relatively short, I still took the opportunity to ease back into some overdue sleep.

The only thing that really surprised me on my return to society was that Jeff's unusual garb was not considered strange by the other passengers. In fact, his suit was the rule and Lew and I the exceptions.

Of course, I was asleep too quickly to worry much about it.

11

"How Do You Do, Mr. Director?"

A rough hand shook my shoulder. "Come on, Augie boy, New York."

I cracked my eyes to see Jeff standing over me with that sadistically wide smile that early risers reserve for late sleepers. With all of the warm friendship I could muster, I answered, "Up yours."

"Eli!" came Holly's urgent whisper from my left side. "We're back in *civilization* now! You'll *have* to watch your language!"

"Sorry, teacher." I stretched and stood.

Outside the windows of the train, the world's largest city flowed in the light of a new day. It had once contained fifteen million people, and now held only a fifth of that number, yet it boasted almost five hundred thousand more than Shanghai, the next most populous.

I had never seen the city before my capture and must have seemed like the classic yokel as I left the train. A flash of one of my last "daydreams" recurred as I stared openmouthed at one of the tallest manmade structures I had ever seen, and it matched my artificial memory down to the last, distantly tiny windows. I felt that I should walk down the blocks that separated me from its looming magnificence and seat myself at its base, awaiting some sidewalk Freud to pause and lecture me on an obvious inferiority complex.

"Lapsing again?" asked Doc, as he bumped past me in departing the train.

"Huh? Oh, no, not right now," I replied. "But I just missed one heck of an opportunity."

Once out of the depot with our luggage, we assembled in a nearby cafe for a short breakfast and conference. Chuck spoke to us from the head of a large, isolated communal table.

"Okay, folks," he grinned both nervously and happily, "here we are. Jeeze, we're in New York City."

"I hate long dinner speeches," Jeff said out of one corner of his mouth.

"Right. The first thing we have to do is get rid of these papers we're carrying and substitute the second set that Doc so prudently drew up for us."

"Gee," muttered Lew, "I kind of liked being Hiroshi Kuniakaya of Tokyo. It sounded so aristocratic."

"The new papers will kill off the trail left from Albany by the first set. Next we'll have to disperse throughout the city, get living quarters, and try to blend into the local setup. Shana and I will travel as husband and wife so that I can help her contact Congresswoman Barbara Ryan; she is probably our best regional bet for political assistance.

"Doc has calculated that we each have enough money to last for two months of moderate living, providing, of course, that inflation hasn't progressed at an unforseen rate. This, friends, means that we each will have to begin considering finding, if you'll pardon the expression, jobs."

"Oh no!" gasped Jeff, clutching in the general vicinity of his heart.

"Not while we're eating, please!" I added.

Chuck smiled. "I just hope that most of you have more professional qualifications than I," he said.

"Oh sure," answered Ellen. "I can weave the prettiest rain catch that you've ever seen."

Doc produced a thin folder from his single suitcase. "Shall we proceed with the new identities? I have a set for a Mr. and Mrs. Jason Graves that will fit admirably for Chuck and Shana. Here is one for you, Lew, Mr. Sessumu Ohba, Osaka."

Chang took the offered paper and said tiredly, "Would you believe that I had never been outside of New England before I was deported?"

"Who would like to be Burl Truman?"

"Burl?" asked Jeff.

"Sold," said Doc.

"Hey, wait—"

"I'll be Patrick Morrison, and Thumper can be my nephew

135

Bertram. We'll have to see about having some special clothing made. Ellen, would you consider being my mistress from Sacramento? Karen Milner?"

"Kiss me, fool," she answered.

"Ahem, yes, who does that leave?"

"I suppose I should feel slighted," I said, "and I will if you give me a name like Ignatius Obadiah."

"How about Reuben Vincent?"

"Not bad, not Shakespeare, but not bad."

"What about me?" asked Holly.

"Uh... here it is, Susan Davenport, from Aberdeen, Washington."

Linda, eating quietly in Ellen's pocket, said nothing.

"Now that that's settled, I propose that we meet here tomorrow morning at nine to exchange information," Garner said. "Try to get a room with a phone, so we can maintain quick contact, and Shana and I will decide when to approach Ryan."

"Any secret password we can use?" Lew asked. "You know, of course, that W. H. O. controls all of New York and routinely tapes random telephone calls."

"Good point," Chuck agreed. "Okay, if for any reason one of us has to meet with the rest, the phrase will be 'Breakfast at Fourth Corner.'"

We agreed.

Jeff stood and straightened his elaborate costume. "So, good friends, the time has come for our true and loyal company to disperse amidst strong clasps and warm tears, seeking our fates in the uncaring world without. Adieu and adieu."

Doc, Lew, and Chuck rose, but I leaned back and grinned. "And if you leave first, you won't have to pick up the check, correct?"

"Most assuredly, Manduke." With a wide flourish, he placed the outrageous hat on his equally outrageous head, picked up his luggage, and strolled from the restaurant.

"See you tomorrow," Holly-Susan called after him.

I laid a couple of bills before my plate. "An example we would all do well to follow," I said. *"Hasta mañana."*

Trailing the usual wishes of good will, I also passed through the open doors into the morning office traffic. Nostalgia had long been a prime emotion in these post-Plague times, and this was reflected in nothing so much as the clothing of the average citizen. Styles from practically every recorded period in human history were represented as long as they offered sufficient protection against the brisk winter weather. Jeff's Musketeer outfit was inarguably mild when compared to the robes of King Henry VIII or the feminized armor of a Norse Valkyrie. With a private smile, I muttered to myself at the chaotic display of modern regression and turned to my left.

"Where were you planning to start looking for a room, Eli?" asked a girl's voice from behind me.

"Haven't the slightest idea, Holly," I said without turning.

"I guess you'd better call me Susan."

"Only if you call me Reuben, Susie."

"Okay. Mind if I help you look?"

"Why not? Four eyes are better than two, or is that too many eyes spoil the boiling pot?"

We found an acceptable apartment about noon and decided to share it and split the rent. The building manager wasn't overly ecstatic concerning this plan since he, like most other managers in New York, had a huge apartment building with pitifully few tenants, and he even tried to pull an ancient policy requiring proof of marriage before allowing two people of sexes opposite one another to share the same room. But we changed his tune by getting three quarters of the way out of the front door before he was able to stop us.

I slept long and comfortably for most of the day, saw New York by night, rediscovered automotive ground travel, and slept some more. My stomach masterfully dealt with the challenge of attuning from spottily burned animal flesh and raw vegetables to concentrated space mush to this new, semi-nutritional and overly prepared cuisine. By the next morning, it had almost adjusted.

At the Fourth Corner Breakfast, only Thumper was missing (Doc explained that he preferred to remain in the hotel room, watching television and away from the crowds). The most important news to come out of this meeting other than our new addresses was that Congresswoman Ryan and several other possible politically liberal allies would be assembled on the next evening at Lindsay Hall for an official appearance by William Kurtz himself.

I felt that it would be mighty risky to show ourselves at a gathering that would undoubtedly contain a hundred W. H. O. strong arm men, but Shana and Chuck viewed it as a golden opportunity to impart the truth about Kurtz and his "mutant haven" to the most influential people at once. In the rare chance that something did go amiss in our exposition, Chuck suggested that the fewer of us accompanying Shana the better. Since Jeff already looked normal—sort of naturally ugly— and I had fashioned a passable tooth covering from department store denture mold, we could go along as bodyguards. Ellen could also attend for backup help, and Chuck would risk his too obvious profile to supervise matters. The rest would be safely back in their hotel rooms, so that we couldn't all be captured in a single net, anyway.

My formal dress for the occasion consisted of a mid-nineteenth century English gentleman's suit, which the store clerk had assured me was most popular with current political leaders. The vest was too small, the leather shoes too large, and the fluffed cuffs embarrassing, but I wasn't worried about being eye-catching or individualistic, only anonymous.

Shana wore a very expensive full-length gown, and Chuck selected a tuxedo with a hat much like mine and a darn good putty nose. It still looked big, but not pointed. Ellen appeared in a layered dress, jacket, and gloves that effectively integrated her into the norm. An unscheduled accomplice was Holly, who "just *couldn't* stay behind" and wore a covering ensemble that left only her face to hide. She did this by applying a Caucasian tone skin cream that looked fairly natural and promised not to run or smear during the night.

"Here it is almost eight-thirty," Jeff said as we stood outside the large hall on an otherwise deserted corner. Inside, the lights could be seen and the sounds of a good crowd could be heard over the slow December breeze. "Isn't anybody going to say,'Let us pause for a brief moment of meditation before we embark on this final great mission'?"

"Would it help?" Chuck asked.

"Not in my case. I'd need at least six years."

"Shouldn't we have brought Lew along...just in case?" Holly questioned nervously.

"No," Garner assured her. "At these affairs, the alcohol flows like water, and as soon as some half-drunk politician slapped Lew on the back, he'd get about sixteen little bones stabbed into his palm."

"Oh."

I laughed. "Let's just hope that some drunk doesn't get fresh with Ellen and play Columbus with her tail."

"Just let him try," she grinned.

"Be done with this tomfoolery," suggested Jeff. "Are we going in or not?"

"Well, I didn't come forty-five light years to stop *here*," Chuck said, "so I suppose we go in."

Our rather slim hopes of a quiet entrance lay on Shana's status as a Congressman's daughter. As such, she possessed the special identification pass that admitted her to any non-restricted W. H. O. gatherings and, even though Shana was a wanted face on Thear, it was possible that these minor flunkies wouldn't be aware of her unfortunate political condition. If they responded in a threatening manner, it was up to Jeff and me to insure their quiet cooperation.

The taller of the two doormen glanced casually at the pass, while we stood nervously aside, and barely read the name. A portable infrared viewer assured him of its validity.

"Check Miss . . . ah, Wilbanks and her party with the gun and let them in," he told his companion.

The second man dusted us with a device resembling a hand-held movie camera and watched its rear screen for any trace of explosive material, whether it was in a bullet or a cardboard casing. The gun *didn't* register tooth caps, false noses, green skin, or hidden tails, and we passed into the large hall with unvoiced sighs of relief.

"That wasn't so hard," Holly whispered.

"Shana, keep your face down until we can enlist two or three powerful friends. Kurtz wouldn't dare have us killed in front of sympathetic politicians," Chuck said.

"What about along with them?" I asked gloomily.

The auditorium portion of the building was brightly lit from overhead, and the reason became obvious when we saw six large, mobile T.V. cameras.

"We're going to be on television," Jeff said with a smile. "How about that? I make my dramatic debut as the star of a life and death struggle for human dignity."

"Let's mingle," Chuck hissed.

It was apparently some minutes before the speech was to begin, and most of the elite guests were still on their feet, drinking beverages offered by young maids and talking among themselves. A large stage was prepared for its illustrious speaker with a lectern, folding chairs, and a four by four, six foot high, transparent cage containing a nude, teenaged girl. She was a mutant, as evidenced by her four blue eyes, but otherwise she was pretty cute.

"Good God," Chuck mumbled. "Why have they got that poor kid on display like that?"

"She's a visual aid," Ellen answered. "Throughout his speech, Kurtz will refer to her with words and a pointer to illustrate the natural inferiority of a gawf. Nine times out of ten, he uses a young girl. I went through it myself."

"The man has some taste," Jeff commented.

"But it's so degrading," added Holly. "I feel so sorry watching her cry that way."

"Yeah," I agreed. "It's a wonder she doesn't drown."

A male voice broke over the loudspeaker and politely asked the visitors to be seated. Like elegant sheep, we all did.

"See anybody?" Chuck asked as we searched for good seats.

"Only Barbara Ryan," Shana answered with the trace of a smile.

"Where?"

"Second row back in the right section."

We were suddenly trailing behind a rushing Chuck Garner as he pushed ungraciously through the crowd for the few seats surrounding Congresswoman Ryan and her husband. He and Shana slid into the only two vacancies next to her while the other four of us stood awkwardly in the aisle and stared at one another, one of my less favorite pastimes.

James William Kurtz walked onto the stage with no fanfare, but the entire assembly was on its feet and applauding wildly before he reached the lectern. This man, this god of Earth and Satan of Thear, was in my personal sight for the first time in my life, and I saw him as a slender, medium-height white man with coal black hair, a very thin mustache, and an intense, icy gaze. I could have torn him in half before breakfast, yet he controlled me as if I were only so many pounds of soil. I had feared this man in my youth, hated him in middle years, and used his name as a curse on Thear, so it was difficult to accept him as the instigator of his numerous hells.

"Here you are, you bastard," I said as the applause filled my ears.

"Please be seated," Kurtz addressed the crowd over the microphone. His voice was a polished, trained baritone. We found four seats within a row of Ryan and Shana. "To begin, I wish to thank each and all of you for attending this meeting, which, I hope, shall rectify an inadequacy that has been brought to my attention. This is going to be an elementary, but much needed instruction in the basic inferiority of the mutant."

"Just as programmed," Ellen whispered. "I honestly believe the man has an ego problem."

I started to reply, but held up when I saw Chuck lean over to Congresswoman Ryan and, in a low voice, say, "Pardon me, Congresswoman, could I speak to you in private?"

Ryan's slightly startled eyes searched Garner's face for some familiarity, but found none. "Perhaps later—the director is speaking now."

"It involves my companion."

As Ryan watched, Shana pulled the long, dark hair away from her face. Recognition flooded over the woman like a physical wave. "My lord!" she whispered. "Shana! The news sources said that you and Farrell were killed on Thear!"

Chuck made a shushing motion with his lips and finger. "In the hall," he whispered. "We've got some pretty surprising things to tell you."

"Certainly." With outward calm, she rose, waited for our friends to move into the aisle, and then walked from the room. Jeff shot me a raised brow look that asked if we should follow them, but I figured that Kurtz or his men might get suspicious if seven of us left at once, so I shook my head.

We waited, nervously, while Kurtz droned on about the five intrinsic signs of mutation, even when no external deformities were present. He poked the sobbing girl mercilessly with his wooden pointer, as Ellen tensed in rising anger. She had been there. Finally, when he came to the part about freaks being a "clear and defined menace to progressive human society," Jeff and I chuckled audibly. A large lady seated next to me—one of those refined to the point of ridiculousness—gave me a "Young man, no one *laughs* at the director!" expression, so, characteristically, I Bronxed her.

Holly jabbed me with a silken elbow, but she was only getting me to look at Chuck, who now stood at the rear of the room. He was unobtusively gesturing to us.

"Now?" Jeff asked.

I nodded, and we rose and walked back to meet him. I could feel Kurtz' men watching as we stumbled down the crowded aisle into the hall, and I wasn't at all surprised to see four of the same assembled by the front doors, mumbling and laughing to themselves. Ryan, Shana, and Chuck were standing only a few feet upwind of them.

"Here they are," Garner said in a low tone. "Jeff, Ellen, Cat, and Caribou. Congresswoman Ryan has agreed to help us with the, uh, plan we were discussing."

Ryan spoke, "This is it? Your entire group?"

"Kind of disappointing, aren't we?" said Jeff.

"Not at all," she replied. "I just wanted to make sure that you were all here..."

I started to speak up about the absent members but refrained when I saw Chuck shake his head almost imperceptibly. "This is the lot," I told her. "We started out with more, but the trip back was pretty hazardous."

"So," she sighed, "I might as well say what I have to. Shana, you know how I feel about you and Farrell. His death—and the manner of it—was a blow to me, but things . . . have changed since you left. There's nothing I would like more than to secure a lever to work against Kurtz' rule, and, ordinarily, your testimony would be just the point needed, but times have changed."

"What do you mean?" Shana's voice was tense, frightened.

"Before you left, there was still a form of localized power in opposition to W. H. O., but that uprising in Italy two months ago swung the remaining parties into the Kurtz fold."

"Uprising?" Chuck asked.

She nodded. "If there actually was one. The hysterical W. H. O. reports claim that thirty or more undetected teenaged mutants formed an execution squad in Rome and killed almost fifty innocent people before W. H. O. patrols wiped them out in a deserted restaurant."

"This report, coupled with the story of you and Farrell being slain just about finished any organized opposition to the Kurtz doctrine. My position is little more than a figurehead."

"That's terrific," Chuck muttered. "We came forty-five light years to find this."

Ryan shook her head slowly and stepped away from our disconsolate group. "It's really obscene that this madman can perpetrate a myth like Thear and sentence harmless children to hell while deceiving their parents into condoning it." She backed further away. "And do you know what's worse? The fact that I have to score points with the man by betraying friends like you. Guards, arrest them!"

We must have looked like entrants in a mouth-dropping contest as the four men drew their weapons and surrounded us. We had questioned Shana's loyalty, which held up, but never the reaction of the political "friends," and because of this slip, we stood trapped at the end of our bloody journey.

Then Ellen screamed and leaped at them.

She could only thank her lucky stars that the guard who fired was carrying a stunner. She was blasted into unconsciousness while in mid-air, but inertia carried her body into the man and knocked him against the wall. For lack of a better plan, I leaped into the air some fifteen feet and grasped the chandelier. It tore loose in my hands, raining plaster on those below, and plunged the hall into almost total darkness.

Shouts from below were accompanied by slashes of blue flame that cut the blackness around me as I dangled precariously from the ceiling. The chandelier had just enough rooting left to hold me. More loud voices from the speaker's room told me that help would soon arrive for the confused guards, and this wouldn't improve my position in the slightest. I dropped.

I hit the carpet hard and at first wasn't sure that the booming of a gun hadn't just been my skull saying hello to the floor. But when it sounded again and was followed by a scream of pain, I knew I wasn't punchy. A body hit me, twisted, and landed a sweet left hook on the right side of my jaw.

"Ow!" I howled.

"Ooooo!" squealed a female voice. "I broke my hand! I broke my hand!"

Cursing, I stumbled up and pushed in the direction I hoped would lead to the door. A dark shape before me extended an arm, and another roar from a gun greeted me. The bullet missed, but I didn't, kicking his legs from under him and hurrying by.

"Cat!" Jeff's voice called out. "I've got Ellen! Where are you?"

A blue streak answered him.

"Dadblast it!" He yelled, ducking.

The door burst open and a human shape was silhouetted there briefly, dashing out before anyone could take aim. I headed for the same destination along with three other faceless forms, but I beat them through and stationed myself just outside the huge doors. The next person out was Shana, and I let her rush past. The second was a guard that I thumped. Third came Jeff with Ellen across his right shoulder.

"You're mighty selective," gasped a voice, Chuck's, from behind me.

"Part of the job," I said, while punching another guard. Barbara Ryan pushed her head tentatively out and quickly withdrew it upon seeing me.

"We're all out . . ." started Jeff. Then he shouted, "Caribou, will you get your little tail out there."

She appeared, badly frightened and holding her gloved left hand against her stomach. "I think I broke my hand," she shuttered.

Pulling the door shut, I wrapped a purloined belt through the two heavy handles and tied it securely. I finished just as a high caliber bullet smashed through a panel no more than a foot from my head.

"Let's go!" Chuck said.

"Well put," I added.

We ran across the street to a parked auto, which was useless since we had no key, but Garner, stumbling, led us right by it to a public transport. It was bill-activated and designed to seat twelve, so there was plenty of room as we tumbled in.

"A dollar!" I shouted from behind the wheel. "Somebody give me a dollar!"

Jeff pulled a ten from his breast pocket and handed it to me, saying, "You realize, of course, that I expect change?"

"Give me your name and address, sir, and I'll mail—"

"Will you two *shut up*?" Chuck screamed.

I slipped the bill into the appropriate slot, and the machine hummed to life. Because I was probably the worst driver of the group, I was the chauffeur, slapping the vehicle into drive and squealing into the street. The front door of the building was being pounded savagely, and ominous sounds were bubbling from the rear, so no one commented on my exceeding lack of propulsive skill.

I wasn't surprised that I smashed the transport into another car before we had gone a hundred feet. What did surprise me was that the accident wasn't my fault, because the other vehicle had flashed out of the alley next to Lindsay Hall and darted right in front of me. When we hit, the second car was damaged the worse and knocked onto the sidewalk by the forward motion of our heavy bus. We suffered nothing more devastating than a couple of bumped heads and a renewal of pain in Holly's hand.

"Chuck, look!" shouted Jeff from almost at my side. "Look who's getting out!"

A pair of W. H. O. uniformed guards were slumped unconscious in the front seat of the car, but the passenger was unhurt and stepping from the rear door of the wreck. He was slender, of medium height, and had dark black hair.

"Kurtz!" Garner roared in surprise. "Grab him, Cat, before he can get away!"

Leaving the idling bus, I charged out and around to meet the slightly dazed man with wide open arms, and Jeff was right behind me. As Kurtz tried to focus on me, I said, "How do you do Mr.

144

Director sir? My name is Harper, and I'm from Thear."

He suddenly looked startled and turned to run, but Jeffrey Nichols, also of Thear, calf-tackled him with considerable gusto. "You don't really want to leave us so quickly," Jeff assured him, laughing. "So, if you'll be so kind as to get up..."

Kurtz lay still, eyes closed.

Jeff spoke with a bit more vehemence, "Come on, you bastard, get up!"

No response.

I stooped and rolled the body over, while Jeff placed a hand on his shoulder to pull him up. Nichols stopped and stared at me. "Hey, Cat," he said, "I think maybe I hit him too hard."

The body was just that, a body. With no discernible heartbeat or breath, I could only come to one conclusion, which I admitted when I said, "He's as cold as a cube, Jeff."

"I killed him," marvelled the other. "I killed J. W. Kurtz! Uh, is that good?"

"I don't know," I said. "It depends on who the next guy on the political totem pole turns out to be. God, I hope it isn't Barbara Ryan."

Chuck stuck his head out of a window, and we explained the situation. "Then come on," he told us. "Let's clear out of here until we can see how matters stand."

"Should we bring the body?" I asked.

A shot rang out from the W. H. O. men rounding the large hall.

"Damn the body!" said Jeff with feeling.

We dodged back into the bus, and I jerked it down into reverse. Backing away from the wreck site, I pulled around the ruined limousine just in time for Holly to scream out piercingly.

"He got up!" she proclaimed.

My eyes confirmed this, as I saw the recently lifeless body of James William Kurtz walk quickly from the spot he'd died upon and direct the arriving security guards to our departing bus. "I'll be damned," I whispered.

"Drive!" Chuck yelled.

I drove.

We lost the pursuers in the first bus, abandoned it (because it could easily be located by the company that owned it), walked three dark blocks, and commandeered another. By the time we reached the outskirts of the city, we felt temporarily safe from Kurtz' men, even though tired, defeated, and confused. I still couldn't believe my memory of the director's resurrection, because I had been so sure that he had been dead and not unconscious or faking it. There had been *no* heartbeat at all.

Ellen was awake by then and able to walk, so we wordlessly decided to leave the second bus and walk to a meeting place where we could summon the rest. The hounds would be after our skin following the utter failure we had encountered, and we needed to make some sort of plans. But, when we left the vehicle, we were one short.

"Chuck," I called into the dark interior. "Do you propose to join us?"

"Cat," he called back weakly. "Come in here a minute."

"What's the matter?" I asked on finding him lying on one of the seats.

"I was hit, Cat, when the lights were out, and I've come about as far as I can." His voice was low and quivering.

I felt his stomach with one hand and touched a large wet spot. "You've been bleeding the whole time, haven't you?"

"Umm," he grunted affirmatively.

"Hey, man, why didn't you *say something*?"

"What good would it have done? This was bad; it needed a doctor, and you know there's not a doctor in this town who would touch one of us."

"What do you mean, 'needed'? It still does, and we'll get you one." Saying this, I started to lift him.

"No, no," he protested, "let me lie here. It hurts to move and, as corny as it may sound, I know it won't be too much longer."

My own voice was deeply solemn. "It's really that serious, then?"

"Yeah, really. I want to . . ." he grunted in sudden pain. "I want to talk to you a minute. This is a hellava time for me to check out, with you guys in this mess."

"You didn't schedule it, man."

"That's right. But, Cat, you've got to help them. I've known you'd be the only one to take over since we started this thing, that's why I've been so rough on you at times, trying to teach you. Your best . . . best bet is to scatter now, hide in the cities, but you'll have to do it orderly, not in panic. Have Doc draw up some perfect papers, disguise . . . yourselves. Maybe someday . . . soon, the end will come for this . . ."

"I'm no leader, Chuck," I said. "You know I'm not."

"You're the best . I've got, Cat," he responded. "Don't let me

146

down now. Hold them together, at least until you're all safely hidden."

"But, Chuck—"

A familiar smile lit his dark face. "Hey, it stops hurting, did you know that? I don't see any angels or hear music or nothing, but it doesn't hurt anymore."

I spoke dryly, like snapping twigs. "This is it?"

"I don't know . . . I've never done it before . . . I guess so. I don't have anything to compare it to." He sighed heavily, but with great pleasure. "At least I didn't die over there, Cat—oh, God, I'm almost there . . . no flashbacks . . . no pain . . . I can't talk, really . . . the words don't . . . if you only knew what's . . . sweet Jesus, here I go . . . Max Baer . . ."

And he was dead. Number seven. The man who had dreamed it. A man with no special abilities, but who led us from the primal depths of human degradation to one glorious shot at redemption. And he lay still before me in a cold, silent bus.

"'Max Baer,'" I repeated, wondering what he had meant. Then it slowly came to me from the foggy recesses of my memory. It was in a book cataloguing the last words of famous people in history. With his dying breath, former Heavyweight Champion Max Baer was claimed to have said, quite simply and fully, "Oh, God, here I go!" Charles Garner was in good company.

As I carried him from the bus to meet the others, I was an old, old man.

That was it for Shana. While I called the rest from a public booth to tell them of our failure, she sat on a cold bench under a yellow street light, rubbing Chuck's still face. Of all the mutants she had been forced to associate with, she had come closest to liking Garner because of his continual fairness and honesty. She once said that he had remained the "most civilized" of us and described briefly how he had helped her accept the loss of her father.

And now Chuck Garner was dead, killed by one of her own kind. It was more than Shana could take, so there would be no more campaigns for liberation, no more futile pleas with now unsympathetic friends. She was going underground.

Doc advised us to join him and the others at his leased cabin at a motel just five miles away, reasoning that we could enter without being seen and have a few hours to plan our next move. "Plan," he had said. How could you plan your own part in a rout?

Even though there were nine people in the five rooms, the air was oppressive with silence, as we sat eating or sipping coffee. The television set was on, but the sound was off. Chuck's body, which we couldn't leave behind, was on the bed in one of the two bedrooms.

"What do we do, Cat?" asked Jeff with as dull and lifeless a voice as I had ever heard him use.

"Shana's going to get out of town in the morning; she'll head west. With any luck, she should be able to hide from Kurtz, for a while, anyway," I answered partially.

"Okay, what about the other eight of us?"

Holly had washed the makeup from her face and was massaging the jammed, but unbroken knuckles of her left hand. I had an idea that she wouldn't be punching me in the head again any time soon. "I think we should all do that. We certainly can't fight the government, and it would be much safer," she said.

"Strange," Doc reflected, "but most of the existing mutants could live quietly on Earth following a little cosmetic surgery, amputations, electrolysis, *et cetera*. Of course, this wouldn't affect the genetic changes, and a high percentage of the mutations have been shown to be transmittable—"

"Shh!" I said suddenly. "Turn up the television, quick!" I had seen a "bulletin" flashed on the screen.

"...are asked to watch for the following fugitives in the New York vicinity," the telecast said. An old capture photo of Chuck appeared. "Charles Emilio Garner, government designation L381-65597, age twenty-five, height five feet nine inches..." The announcer went on to describe myself, Shana, Thumper, Ellen, Doc, Lew, Mike Bolger, Linda, and Holly. The description of Thumper was totally oral, with no given number or proper name, just estimated height, weight, and age.

"Eli, how do they know all about us?" Holly asked with an amazement we all felt.

Before I could answer, Jeff added, "And why did they give only the ones who made it off of Thear? Why Chuck and Mike?"

"Beats me," I said.

"That's eerie," Lew commented. "I'll bet they know right where we are, right now."

"What are we going to do?" asked Ellen.

The others looked at me.

Almost predictably, my harried brain withdrew from the pressures and responsibilities, and I lapsed. I was walking into a large building, a cathedral, and it was late at night. Deep within the structure, I found a big room lit with hundreds of candles and filled with angry adults wearing black robes. One individual spoke over the murmuring of the rest and pushed forward three small children, mutants. Before my disembodied eyes, the cursing mass of terrified humanity beat two tiny girls and a boy to death with their hands.

"Eli?"

I grunted. "All right, I know what to do, and it's the only thing we can do other than run. I want everyone to listen closely, because there's not only a possibility, there's a probability that most of us will die. You can decide if you want to help me or not. Doc, where does Kurtz live?"

12

"Into the Valley"

A lot of things were still missing from post-Plague Earth, both good and bad. One of the missing bad things that no one particularly wanted to see reappear was the unbalanced pyromaniac known as the firebug. On the last Thursday morning before Christmas, 2029, the firebug returned to human society with a vengeance.

The huge city no longer utilized all of its long-developed boundaries, and large sections lay abandoned and boarded off. One such area was in Manhattan, just north of the Brooklyn Bridge and extending up to the Midtown Tunnel. Traffic passed through this quiet section, people didn't actually avoid it, but no one lived there and no work was conducted. Lew, Jeff, Ellen, and I burnt it down.

Striking quickly in the early hours, the four of us broke into tens of buildings and torched their ground floors to further a plan that admittedly bore little hope of success. The unused portion of the city would be destroyed with little danger to human lives, but fear that it would spread uncontrollably would effectively monopolize all of the local W. H. O. employees. Some firemen would die, possibly, but the World Health Organization had declared war on us, and misplaced sympathy had to be put aside.

Many of the fires went out of their own accord, but enough lived and grew to accomplish our purpose. By six that evening, we sat around the television in Doc's lodge and watched the progress of our raging child.

"How much longer, Cat?"

I looked up at Ellen from the couch and answered, "Give it an hour. By then, most of Kurtz' men should be fighting the fires."

"If we're lucky."

"Why should we presume to rely on luck now?" Doc asked rhetorically.

Holly, trying to lift our blackened spirits, said, "At least Shana and Linda are safe. If they had been caught by the guards at the depot, we would have heard about it by now, wouldn't we? Eli?"

"No question. The way last night's telecast described her as 'a traitorous, patricidal radical,' if they'd caught her boarding the train, the newspaper would be running four special editions an hour."

She smiled hopefully.

It had been a year and a half since I had seen or spoken to any member of my family, last glancing at them among the thousands assembled on the landing field the day I was shipped to Thear. Now, on what I felt was possibly the eve of my death, I recognized a painful longing slowly arising. While the rest watched the fire, I silently walked into the next room, Chuck's resting place, and cleared the screen on the telephone. The buttons at its base felt strange, as I punched out my home number, and I wondered if news of my arrival had spread that far.

Suddenly Lew stood at the doorway. "Hey, maybe you shouldn't do that, Cat. Kurtz' men might be tapping into the line," he pointed out.

I spoke in a low voice, "The hell with Kurtz' men."

"Well put," said Jeff from behind him. "I think we should all use the opportunity. When you're finished, of course, Cat." They left.

The phone's screen blended from a featureless white into the browns and shadows of a room. I recognized the room as one in the home I'd lived in most of my life before leaving for college. In answer to the phone's chimes, a young, brown-haired girl appeared.

"Hello?" she said.

"Beth? God, I never thought I'd see you again!"

Her face lit. "Eli? Eli, is that you? Mom! Mom, it's *Eli!*"

I laughed. At fifteen, my little sister had surely changed in looks, but that "Mom!" remained as shrill and familiar as ever.

"He's home!" she was shouting.

My mother's upper body joined her in the screen, and though the disbelief was evident in her eyes, it was quickly replaced. "Oh baby! Where are you? Are you—are you here?"

"I'm in New York, Mom. Eleven of us made it back a few days—"

"Are you pardoned?" She was joined by three more eager faces, my brothers and other sister. "Did the council repeal your conviction?"

I tried to grin. "No, Mom, we stole a ship."

"You stole a ship? Elias, they'll be after you!"

"They are."

"Can you get home? We'll hide you here, get you out of the country somehow!"

"No, I can't, Mom; I have something to do."

"Why not? You'll be safe here, son!"

I hesitated. Why not indeed? I didn't want to die, that was for sure, but I did want to kill James William Kurtz for what he had done to me and all of the others. Still, if I had time to rest and make plans... "Let me talk to Dad," I said.

Beth choked and ran from the screen, as the rest dropped their heads and said nothing. Finally, Mom spoke through spilling tears, "You don't know, do you? You couldn't."

"What?"

"After... after you left, the man... Kurtz' men arrested him for obstruction of justice and hiding you. They said he tried to... escape..."

"No." My right fist rose above a heavy, oaken table. "No, no, *no!*" I hit down at it once, twice, and it crashed to the floor in splinters. "Oh my Lord, why this, too?" Stumbling into the wall, I knocked a gaping hole in the paneling.

"Eli," Mom called from the phone, "please come home to us."

Cold pain drove the irrational anger from me like a wind, and I straightened myself before the screen. "I can't come back, Mom, I've got to kill a man. I love you. Goodbye."

"Don't go now, Eli—"

I cut off the connection.

"Bad news, eh?" Jeff said, entering the room and seeing the damage.

"He's dead, Jeff," I answered in a croaking voice. "Kurtz killed my father. I'm going to tear that son of a bitch apart with my hands."

I walked from the room, and the others followed to use the phone; most of their conversations were like mine. Only Thumper failed to make a call. Maybe he didn't have anyone, or maybe he couldn't remember them.

Holly spoke last and very briefly. She left the room crying because, as I had accidentally heard, her parents had ordered her to turn herself in to the "proper authorities." It was a sad night all around.

That Kurtz' permanent home was in the recently constructed labyrinth underneath what used to be called Rockefeller Center, Doc told us, was common knowledge. That it was heavily guarded and bomb proof was even commoner knowledge. But another important bit of information concerned the fact that all local civil services were peopled with W. H. O. members, and, with our manufactured inferno eating its hungry way north, we hoped that only a token guard would be left at the Center.

The eight o'clock darkness veiled our movements, as we walked in disguise along the virtually deserted Fifth Avenue. There were seven out of the original seventeen still actively in the battle, and higher thoughts of noble achievements had totally forsaken us to be replaced by vengeance and hatred. Thumper, who had been withdrawn and quiet since arriving on Earth, was now alive and primed with anticipatory excitement.

"Well," whispered Jeff, as we paused before the Fifth Avenue entrance, "do we just blunder blindly in and meet with success equal to that in Lindsay Hall?"

"That's the idea," I replied. "With the guards out fighting campfires, I hope we can make our way past the skeleton force and get to Kurtz."

"Brilliant tactical mind," he muttered, "simply brilliant."

The main building in this portion of the Center was a single story, wide affair with countless glass panels and cool, indirect lighting. It appeared to be empty as we entered in pneumatic silence and surveyed the scene.

"Doc?" I asked.

"Any down escalator should take us to the next level. After the remodelling done in '21, Kurtz had at least three subsurface levels outfitted for his private use."

The first escalator we came to was just inside the inner lobby, and it was activated, so, lining up in an orderly fashion, we took it. The first guard also was near the escalator, at its bottom, in fact. He seemed congenial, though surprised at encountering visitors so late.

"Sorry, folks," he smiled at us. "No one beyond this point. If you'll just take the next escalator—"

"But we have a special pass," said Jeff, while he made a dramatic search of his vest for the non-existent note.

"A pass?"

"Yes, sir, it should be . . . ah, here it is." Saying this, he made as if to present the man with the pass, but punched him with a good right, instead. The guard stumbled back against the wall, where Lew clipped his temple with a knockout blow. "Damn," hissed Jeff, shaking his hand, "they *are* making them like they used to!"

I looked at the empty hallway we now occupied and noticed that it was closed off by two metal doors. Lew quickly searched the fallen man, but came up with only a rectangular piece of plastic that resembled an identification card.

"Do you suppose this is a key?" he asked.

"Let's find out." I pressed the card against an outline of equal size next to one of the doors. It fit perfectly, and a little red light glowed into life above it, but the door remained closed.

"Seems to perform some sort of service," Doc said. "Perhaps it released the lock or neutralizes an alarm, but the door must be activated by some palm code or arithmatic combination."

"Really?" I asked. Still holding the card in place, I raised my left leg and kicked the door in. "Too bad we don't have the secret to it; I really think we could have gotten Kurtz tonight."

Ellen and Lew gaped at the smashed door.

"No alarm, apparently," Doc added. "I believe the card cuts out the circuit. Hold on to it."

We went through into another corridor, this one long and dotted with closed doors on either side. No one appeared to greet us, so we retrieved the unconscious guard's stunner and handcuffed him to the escalator. Cautiously, we proceeded.

These doors all opened to our touch, but they didn't help our search, being openings to empty rooms. We counted twelve cells before the corridor doglegged to the right. More empty rooms.

"This level could stretch out for a mile or more, Cat. Shouldn't we split up to cover more ground?"

I didn't answer Ellen's question immediately, because a new mental feeling seemed to have invaded me as I stood there. It was like standing close to an invisible fire and sensing its danger by the heat on your skin. It was in the bottom of my mind, if you can realize such a sensation, and it led me to believe that there was danger near, below. "No, we stick together for now. We'll go down at the next escalator."

"But we're not finished with this level, yet."

"If there's nothing down there, we'll check again."

The second descent was made in the same manner as the first, except that Thumper shouldered the door in while I held the card in place. This time a guard awaited us on the other side, and he was quicker in recognizing us than his previous companion. His gun exploded as the metal door burst inward, and Thumper took a bullet somewhere in his abdomen before he could react. But, as the rest of us dodged back, the little ape man roared and launched himself on the guard like an animal. The guard screamed, but not very long.

"You okay?" I gasped as the killer stood from the body.

"Thumper okay," he said, not even breathing hard.

"I do believe that there is something on this floor," Jeff commented.

Holly pushed up to my side and said in a low voice, "We have to go back, Eli. There'll be more guards in here, and Thumper's hurt."

At the sound of his name, Thumper bared his teeth in a grin, slapped the rapidly reddening hole in his shirt without wincing, and mumbled, "Hell, come on."

I stepped over the dead man and led them on. Opening the first door on the right side of the corridor, we were met with the hot mustiness of recent habitation in the unlit room. Discarded clothing lay on the floor, I could see a dinette in one corner with food on it, and, had I paid attention to my aroused senses, I would have known who had so recently been there. Thumper sniffed the air and rumbled to himself; he knew.

"Anybody here?" Jeff asked.

Lew walked cautiously into the black doorway that led to the second room and entered it. Touching the illuminating panel, he lit the bedroom to provide for a better look, but I don't believe he was expecting the sight that was revealed. "Good grief!" he barked.

We hustled to the doorway and saw what had startled him so: the bedroom was a chaotic jungle, and on the bed lay Shana Wilbanks. She was swollen and discolored, her face beaten almost beyond recognition, and, nude, she was chained to the bed by one ankle. Holly rushed forward, and Shana tried to sit as we entered. She managed to rise only to one elbow.

"Are you all right?" Holly asked earnestly.

"Get me some water," she rasped in a voice as dry as sand, "please?"

"What happened?" Lew said. "Where did they catch you?"

"On the train. Two men took us off at the first stop."

"Where's Linda?"

"D-dead. She wouldn't let them take her. She killed one man with a dart, but he crushed her when he fell. It was quick."

Ellen stepped to the bed and said tightly, "Who did *this*?"

"Finnegan."

Who else could it have been? Finnegan; missing since the landing, we had dismissed him from our minds and, even though the surrounding air reeked of him, I had ignored my natural alarm until his name was mentioned.

"Have they captured him, too?"

"No, he works for Kurtz." An idea tried to force open the swollen eyelids. "Kurtz is *here*! He stays down the hall!"

Holly arrived with the water, but I held her away until I was finished asking, "Where does he stay?"

"In a room..."

"What room?"

"I think it's 209, or maybe 210."

"Give her the water," I said. "We'll check both rooms—"

"Don't bother," a voice said behind us. "He's in 210."

Finnegan stood nonchalantly in the doorway, arms folded, and smiled at us. He was dressed only in pants, and the lean power of his upper body was all too evident, along with the tangible evidence of Shana's face and trunk. He spat disinterestedly on the floor. "How do you like my new Christmas present? Kurtz really does well by his own."

"He's your employer now?" I asked in a casual tone. "You're being awfully free with information about him."

"Oh, he shouldn't worry at all. See, I'm now his personal bodyguard. I gave him your names, they provided the numbers. Where're Chuck and Bear?"

"Dead."

"Doesn't matter. As for Kurtz' safety, I don't think the lot of you idiots can get through me to him."

Thumper growled and stepped forward on all fours, ape-like. Finnegan tensed and watched him closely.

"What's the matter?" I asked baitingly. At a hand signal, Jeff produced the stolen stungun and carefully took aim from behind my shielding body. "Thumper's just trying to be friendly, aren't you, Thump?"

"Friendly," he grunted.

"You sawed-off throwback," Finnegan growled. "Come on. And then I want you, Cat, just me and you."

Jeff leaped out and shot the stunner with one motion, and, as a consequence, missed. But it's hard to believe that he would have scored had he been on target, so swiftly did the Irishman duck back into the other room. Just as swiftly, he produced a gun of his own and shouted, "Drop it or I'll blow your heart out!"

Jeff held the stunner evenly, but I knew Finnegan would shoot, so I told him to drop it. As slyly quick as ever, he dropped the gun on its opened power pack, and it flared in a brief blue flame before settling into scrap. "Darn," he said, "I'll bet they charge me with that."

"What the hell," Finnegan laughed, tossing his gun aside. "This one ain't loaded."

With a grim smile, Lew Chang sprang before the man and assumed the most business-like of his fighting positions. "Whenever you're ready, Irishman," he said.

I interrupted, "Lew, I'll handle—"

"No, Cat, you and the others need to get Kurtz before the ass gets away again. You and Finnegan and Thumper are tremendous fighters, physically, but you're undisciplined, unrefined. I always knew I could kill any one of you in unarmed combat."

"Shit, that ain't confidence, that's craziness," Finnegan chuckled.

"Maybe," replied Chang. Lightning-like, he staggered Finnegan with a sidekick to the face. "And maybe not."

"I think he can do it," Jeff admitted. "Let's go!"

As the two battled in the outer room, we rushed past them into the hall and headed to our right. Room 210 was there near the end of the corridor, unprotected, as patternly anonymous as the others, and too quiet. I motioned to the others to silently line up on either side of the door, while I kicked it and leaped aside. Sure enough, as it clanged inward, a burst of automatic gunfire spat out at us and ricocheted in ear-splitting cadence around the metal walls of the underground hall.

Doc was hit. With a single yelp of pain, he clutched his right leg with all four hands and bit down on his lip to stifle the moans. The bullets stopped coming and those still careening about whined down the corridor. In the quiet that followed, every breath was a rushing whirlwind.

Okay, I told myself, you're the boss now, what do you do? Charge in? And you'll get your stupid head shot to hell. Wait? Yeah, wait and they'll come to you.

"You out there! Step to the door with your hands up!" shouted a man within the room.

We waited, quietly.

"You heard me!"

Nothing.

Another subdued voice said, "Maybe he's dead. Maybe you got him."

"Sure," answered the first man. "I'll see."

157

Just as I had expected, he poked the barrel of the gun out before him, and, speeded up, I was able to grab it, jerk it into a ninety degree angle, and pull the trailing man out with it. I threw him against the opposite wall, as Jeff kneed the second in the throat when he stuck his head out.

They were the only guards, but the room wasn't empty. With Ellen helping Doc hop in behind, we slowly filed into the practically bare cubicle and looked at James William Kurtz, closeup, for the second time. He stood unarmed and against a wall, looking scared.

The sight, the smell, everything was just as I had remembered it from the previous night, but it wasn't completely right. The heat, the enemy still seemed to be below me.

"Hello, Kurtz," said Jeff, "I'm V110-713392 according to your files, and I can change my skin color." In rapid succession, he went from white to blue to green to red and back again. "Because of this, you have elected that I am not fit to dwell among 'pure' human beings. Perhaps you'd like to explain to me the clear, rational reasoning behind this."

Kurtz spoke in a high, nervous tone. "It's not too late for you to surrender. These men aren't dead, and the penalty won't be—"

Ellen slapped his face sharply, screaming, "You killed Hadji!" Her nails were clawing for his throat as he turned to run. I stepped over to block his flight.

Jeff laughed. "Poetic justice."

Suddenly Kurtz stiffened between us, his eyes rolled back, and his tongue protruded from his mouth. As we watched, he drew back on his heels like a woozy boxer and began to jerk spastically.

"You're not dying yet!" shouted Ellen, holding him erect by the shirtfront.

Kurtz responded with great gasps of air.

"He's having a fit!" Jeff declared.

"Epileptic," Doc corrected him, "obviously a *grand mal* seizure—"

Kurtz dropped heavily to the floor and lay still. My rising feeling of anger and frustration was confirmed when Doc, after a quick examination, slowly said, "No respiration, no heartbeat. I'm afraid James William Kurtz is dead."

Ellen began crying, Thumper merely sat down and stared, Holly hugged close to me, and Jeff muttered in a low, tired voice, "So it ends with a heartattack."

But the evil was still there, gnawing. "Wait, wait a minute."

"He's dead, Cat," said Doc. "We've got to worry about getting out of here."

"I said wait!"

Silence fell, as the six of us stood in the small room and stared at a motionless body on the floor. Two minutes passed in tense quiet, and I was beginning to get the looks from the others when Kurtz coughed. He choked loudly, shuttered, and started to fight in noisy breaths.

"Good Lord, he's alive!" Doc shouted.

Kurtz seemed to gain control of his lungs and managed to sit up, still shaking. "He tried to kill me," the Director said weakly. "I was smothering..."

"What the hell is this?" Jeff demanded.

Kurtz looked up at him and all of us. "Who are you? What are you people doing here?" Upon seeing Holly, he said, "You're green!"

In anger, Jeff lifted the man clear off the floor and shook him. "It's too late, you bastard! You can't pull crap like that now!"

Kurtz' voice was practically a scream. "I'm not him, I swear!"

"Are you Kurtz?"

"Yes, yes, but—"

"Then you're the one I want!"

"Stop!" I snapped at Jeff. "He's telling the truth."

Kurtz babbled, "Sometimes, when he sleeps, I can get out for a while, but he tried to kill me this time!"

"Who?" asked Ellen viciously.

"I don't...I don't know, my gosh, it's been like this for years!"

"Damn, Cat, you don't believe this bull?" said Jeff.

"The hell I don't. This is not the one."

"Your mind again?" Doc asked knowingly.

"Yes," I nodded, "and the real enemy is still below us. How's your leg?"

"Not bad. The bullet missed the bone and major arteries, but there is some bleeding, and I can't walk too well."

I retrieved one of the machine guns belonging to the unconscious guards and gave it to him. "You stay here and watch this guy in case he 'reverts.' If anyone else comes through the door, put a warning blast through their legs."

"All right."

"The rest of you can help me look for the next way down."

Leaving the two of them inside, we took the right passage and ran down the empty hallway. It was two more right turns before we came upon another stairway, this one stationary. It had another metal door at its bottom. The door resisted my desperate kicks, and it took the combined power of shoulders, belonging to Thumper,

Ellen, Jeff, and myself to batter it open enough to squeeze through.

We were cautious this time, but no armed guards greeted us. In fact, testing the air, I could detect no recent human passage. The corridor looked like the others, except for a single rail that ran down the center of it and had branches at every doorway. Actually, the term "rail" may be misleading; it was more like a flat metal strip insulated on either side by rubberized material. Our indelicate method of entry *did* set off an audible alarm.

"Sounds like a bobcat with a torch up his tail!" Jeff yelled above the noise. "No offense, Cat! Which way do we go?"

"Both," I shouted back. "Whoever's down here knows we are, too, so you, Ellen, and Thumper go that way; Holly and I will try this one! And be careful!" I pointed to the countless round lenses spaced every five feet along the tops of the walls. "You'll be watched all the way!"

"Aut vincere aut mori!" Jeff laughed.

I shook my head and grinned. "Why can't you just say 'check' or 'aye aye'?"

"And be so pedestrian?"

We split up, Holly and I going to the left.

Racing down the hall, we were acutely aware of the eyes that were undoubtedly staring down on us, but if we smashed the lenses, the watchers could trail us by the progressive blindness of their cameras. We found the going far too slow, as I had to stop and kick open every door we came to just to check the rooms. All were empty, containing various libraries, laboratories, communication areas, and related equipment. But in one, we did find a projectile handgun with two bullets in the chamber. I gave it to Holly.

"I-I can't use a gun, Eli," she said, holding the huge, deadly piece of metal in both small hands. "I don't know how."

"You point this end at whatever you want to kill and squeeze this trigger. Aim for the chest; you'll have a better chance of hitting."

"It's not only that, I . . . well, I just don't think I could shoot anybody."

Abruptly, the shrill alarm stopped like a choked off scream. It rang on in our ears and gave me a dead feeling in the pit of my stomach.

"That can mean a couple of things," I said.

"What?"

"It's possible that the other three have found whoever we're looking for and killed him, or, and I'll be honest about it, it's more likely that Jeff and Ellen and Thumper are dead. If that's true, he or she probably thinks all of the invaders have been taken care of."

"Oh, no, do you really think they've been killed?"

"I don't want to, but I don't know. Maybe this enemy is so sound a sleeper that the alarm just now woke him. You see, Holly, we're not playing games here. This person knows we're here for blood, and, unless we react rationally, it'll be our blood that we find. You'll shoot."

She didn't answer, walking slowly from the room with head down. I started to follow her when her body came flying back in to land on the floor before me. Blood was pouring from her lips.

"She didn't shoot me, Cat, and I don't think you will," said a familiar voice.

Stepping over her, I headed for the door, only to stop short when a tall, lean figure appeared from the hall holding the pistol. Finnegan.

"You didn't *really* think I was dead, did you?" he leered. "No sir, I wouldn't dream of checking out of this life without saying goodbye to my old friends. One of our other acquaintances did, though." Using his left foot, he kicked a large, roughly round object into our view.

Holly screamed and I snapped my face away, eyes closed. The object was the severed head of Lew Chang.

"Damned good fighter," Finnegan went on. "Fast and tricky. Said he always thought you were better than me at the rough stuff. Of course, I had to kill him, just like I'm going to have to kill you." He looked down at Holly. "And you, baby, later."

I needed time and distraction, so I began to talk. "And like the brave little boy that you are, you're going to shoot us down, is that it?"

He looked at the gun in mock surprise. "Shoot you? Hell, no!" He tossed it noisily back into the hallway. "See, I've always known that I was the better of us two, and to prove it it'll just be one on one, no sidearms."

The moment had come. I had seen it that day outside Vega's hut, but I had always hoped that something would prevent it, because, frankly, Finnegan was one of the strongest, fastest, most vicious and cunning men I'd met on Thear or anywhere else. The prospect of going all out against him chilled me like a breath of Arctic air. Still, I had to keep him talking, and get Holly in a position to go after the gun.

"The main event in your mind, right? You've got to prove yourself *to* yourself by killing me in an equal fight."

"That's right, ass."

"That's stupid, Finnegan. If you're going to kill a man, you stack the deck in your own favor. How do you know I'm not a little faster, a little stronger? Are *you* ready to die?"

He grinned toothily and moved into the room, as I backed slowly away. "Why don't you let me worry about that? You just think of a nice place to be planted, okay?"

"Listen to him talk," I taunted. "You're certainly brave behind words, aren't you? How did you get Lew, a lucky shot? A freak punch at the right time?"

He was out of the door now, completely in the room. Just a little more...

"Sure, that must have been it. Someone like you could never have beaten him in a fair fight unless luck was with you."

"You stinking son of a bitch!" he hissed, walking forward.

"Now, Holly, run!" I shouted. "Get out of here!"

She sat numbly, staring at me through wide eyes.

"I said *run*, stupid!"

She scrambled up and stumbled through the door. It was then that I remembered what I had forgotten to tell her.

"Get the gun!"

Finnegan kicked the door shut behind her and locked it with the inside panel. "I don't think her dainty feet can kick through metal doors as easily as yours can. It's too bad you won't be around to see what I do to your little girl friend before I wring her neck."

A shot whined harmlessly off the door from outside. I could expect no help from Holly. "Why don't you shut up and fight?" I spat.

He was on me like an animal, biting, punching, and kicking. I turned aside the first rush by twisting to my right and making him miss a roundhouse. His fist slammed into the wall with a booming noise, and I hoped he had broken it. But not a sign of pain showed as he renewed his attack.

I had always enjoyed boxing, to my mind the truest of sports, and had spent many hours watching tapes of the Mickey Walkers, the Jack Dempseys, and the Ray Robinsons. Through this, I had picked up a semblance of technique, which I used with success against my maddened foe. Left jabs peppered his bloodying face and right crosses smashed into his jaw and ribs. If I could keep him away, I would have a chance.

But Finnegan was sly, too. In his hands, the furniture of the room became a source of weapons, and a heavy chair crashed into me as I dodged another. He was able to catch me before I could recover my feet, and I was suddenly flying through the air like some weightless toy. When I hit the wall, only the extraordinary strength of my bones kept me from being a shattered target right there.

I was dazed, though, and I had to rouse myself to fully feel the pain of teeth on my throat. He was trying to rip it out! Clutching blindly, I caught an ear and tore it off in my hand so that he drew back, howling in pain. While gasping for my own breath, I managed to kick him in the stomach and get into a standing position. It was a brief respite.

Here we were, engaging in the most savage battle any promoter could dream of, and only the glazed eyes of Lew Chang were there to see it.

The fight continued with Finnegan attacking furiously, using any tactic to gain an advantage, and me punching back in desperation. Before two minutes were gone, we were both bathed in blood, most of it from his torn away ear, and our normal human clothing was holding up like tissue paper. It such a small area, my leaping ability was negated, and he was my equal in speed, so I had to search elsewhere for a weak spot. It was revealed when we were locked together in crushing bear hugs.

Finnegan was strong, as strong as any man I'd ever fought, as strong as Mike Bolger, but I suddenly realized that I was a bit stronger. As his hold around my lungs began to weaken, my own increased, and I could hear the air being forced through his nose and mouth, so I took to pounding his head against the wall until his eyes closed. Then I dropped him.

That was an A-1 mistake. He had no sooner hit than I felt my feet knocked from under me, and I landed solidly on my back. This snarling beast was lashing at me again with all of the fury of a madman. I caught his hands in mine and slowly twisted them outward. I held him at such an inside angle that I was able to break his right wrist before reaching extension.

"Give it up, Finnegan," I gasped as he rolled away.

"Go to hell!" he panted back and leaped at me once more.

It had to end. There was no way Finnegan would lose the fight alive, so when he hit me this time, I caught his body and forced him to the floor. Holding him writhing there, I drew back my fist and hit his rib cage as hard as I had ever hit anything before. You could literally hear the heavy bones as they took the massive blow and, being unequal to the task, broke.

"You bastard," he choked.

I hit him again, and again, and again. Still he struggled, trying to find the one punch that would do to me what I was doing to him. It wasn't until his entire left side was a bloody, pulpy mess that he stopped fighting and collapsed. Sick, hurt, and exhausted, I stood up.

With some unfathomable, unbelievable strength, Finnegan struggled up, sat, and, with the blood pouring from his nose, arched his body back impossibly and snapped it quickly forward, before falling on his face. Finnegan died then, but he had done so in character: he had spat in my eyes.

I was hurting as I lurched toward the door. With broken ribs on both sides, at least one bone fracture in my lower left leg, and numerous weeping cuts, I truly felt like the "walking wounded" of countless old-fashioned war stories. To push on and perform at anything near peak level, I needed twelve hours rest and three or four big meals, neither of which I had any prospect of getting in the immediate future. Wearily, I palmed open the door.

At first, I thought that a dead Finnegan had hit me again in the stomach, as I jerked back five feet and landed in a sitting position. Then I heard the loud booming and felt the shocked numbness begin to give way to livid pain. I had been shot.

Clutching my screaming stomach, I pulled myself erect with an overturned dining table and fell heavily against the wall behind the open door. This treachery, this ultimate treason was almost too much for my jolted mind to accept, but the red running hole was there, and all the proof I would ever need was being rushed to my mind in shockwaves of agony. I *had* been shot.

When the small figure walked cautiously into the room, my bloody right hand was a striking snake that bit its neck, twisted the creature to face me, and lifted it from the floor in trembling rage. A glaze skimmed my eyes, but I forced myself to stay conscious, while I squeezed the life from this green and white thing in my hand.

My vision cleared enough to assure me that that was Holly struggling in my grip, just as I had known it must be. "You damned bitch!" I hurled at her. "You backstabbing little piece of slime! Why did you do it? *Tell me!*"

She couldn't because my fist had trapped the air within her swollen lungs, and soon it would cut the blood to her brain and she would die. But what if she hadn't done it? She wasn't holding a gun. Maybe...

I dropped her in a choking mass at my feet and kicked her in the side to roll her over. "Why did you shoot me?" I demanded. She fought wildly for the breath to speak.

"Eli... Eli, *please!* I didn't... know... I knew Finnegan would win... please..." She was crying by then and holding both of my legs in her arms, pressing her face to my shins. "I-I thought he... would kill you, and if he did... I had to kill *him*! I swear that I didn't know it was... you!"

For a moment, I swayed there, considering the possibility of a lie, but then I really looked at this sad little figure below, and I knew she couldn't be lying. "Get up," I croaked, tasting blood and hoping it wasn't from a lung.

"Please don't hate me, Eli, please!" she continued weeping.

"Come on, we're not out of here, yet." I helped her to stand and almost fell myself.

"Can we leave now?" she asked with wet eyes and cheeks. "You're terribly hurt."

"You want to leave the others down here?"

"No; we'll get them and go!"

I nodded in the direction of the grotesque remnant of our friend. "What about Lew? And Linda? And Mike, and Hadji, and Sheila, what about all of them?"

She couldn't answer.

"It's probably best if you go. You can't help anymore. You're out of bullets, aren't you?"

She nodded.

"Thank God for that. But you know the way, so go back to Doc, and maybe the two of you can make it out alive. I've got to stay here."

"I won't leave you," she whispered.

"I want you to, Holly."

"N-no."

I sighed, bringing new fire to my wounds. "Then, let's go. I'm going to follow my mind from now on, and it tells me that this thing we're after is close to us."

Leaning on her for support, I stumbled into the hall, but she was barely able to carry so much of my weight. "Which way?" she asked.

"The way we were headed."

I didn't stop to kick in any doors, relying instead on the massive feeling of dread and horror slowly building in my brain. This "presence" forced my frightened mind into more frequent lapses of other moments, and I had to fight to control them. We rounded a corner, and about halfway down the hall stood Thumper, on feet and knuckles and bleeding badly from two new wounds on his back.

"Thumper!" Holly shouted.

He knocked on a door with one massive hand. "It in there," he grunted.

"What happened to Jeff and Ellen?"

The ape man gave something equivalent to a shrug. "Who know? Split up back there. I walk into trap with two machine gun. No man."

"You hurt bad?" I asked.

"Yeah," he said frankly. "Die maybe soon. You, too."

"Then we'd both better hurry. Do you think he's in that room?"

"*It* in room. Not man. Thumper more man that *that*. Can smell 'im."

"Let me go, Holly." I stood away from her and faced the door. When Thumper signalled his readiness, our shoulders slammed into it together, and my ribs screamed. Even hurt as we were, our combined power should have smashed the door in a couple of hits, but we had to lunge into it four times before it fell loudly inward.

"Thumper kill!" the massive little man screamed. He leaped into the dark room with wild abandon and charged like a rhino at nothing I could see. About twenty feet into the room, he stepped on a live section of the floor and was suddenly shrieking in anguish, while electric blue light flared around his convulsing body.

"Get out!" I yelled. "Thumper!"

With a great roar, he jerked himself free of the energy and rolled back amid the smell of burning flesh. Holly and I rushed in to his side.

"Oh God for Thumper, God for Thumper," he said weakly. "Bad, Cat, too bad, God for . . ."

With a startling abruptness, the broken door behind us began to crackle with the same energy. It was something more than electricity. Blue flashes of light leaped across the opening, and we were trapped.

"Eli, we can't get out!"

"That's right," agreed a hollow, lisping voice from further in the darkness. "You are trapped, you poor, stupid fools."

I forgot my pain and blood at the sound of this and stood with hair on end and growling. "Who are you?" My voice was barely human.

"Do relax, Mr. Harper," it replied. "You shall discover that shortly."

In agonizing slowness, the lights began to glow overhead, raising the room from black to dim gray, to daylight white. And there, sitting in a sort of motorized wheelchair, was the Thing.

Holly made a sound deep in her throat that might have been a scream had she been any less terror-stricken. I could see her green face take on a pasty, awful color, as she continued to make barely audible and inarticulate grunts. Even I, though warned by its smell what to expect, could think of nothing but running in blind, screaming panic for a moment.

"Dear God in Heaven," I managed to say, "what in the name of sanity are you?"

It looked like a clay model of an adult human being that had been pushed, stretched, and squeezed out of shape. Its head was three times the normal size, while the body was twisted and shrivelled, making it look more like a tail than a trunk. The arms were as slender as pencils, and the hands were long and thin; the legs were useless spiralling little appendages and ended in hooves rather than feet. Not a hair showed on its body, which was partially covered by a yellow sack, and the mouth and nose were grotesquely outsized. It had five, pea-like, lashless eyes.

"Come now, Cat," it chuckled at me, "surely you've seen worse than me on Thear."

"Worse what?"

"Isn't it obvious?" asked the seemingly muscleless creature. "I am like yourself; I am a mutant."

Holly fell against me, shivering, but unable to tear her wide eyes from the horror before them.

"Miss Gylbre, allow me to admit that, despite your unfortunate deformity, you are very attractive," the thing said.

She didn't answer. She couldn't.

In spite of being who I was where I was, I had to laugh in bitter realization. "You're the force behind Kurtz; he's your private puppet, isn't he?"

"That's correct," it said in a voice that reminded me vaguely of Albert Beasley and New Casper.

"And you, *you* started this whole joke about a new society on Thear."

"Of course."

"But you're one of us! I've never seen anyone more deformed!"

"You flatter me. Yes, I'm 'one of you,' since I was born in 1999 and am one of the first, but the facts of my unfortunate birth do not blind me to the harsh and unavoidable realities of life. When I was just a year and a half old, I had already developed mentally to the

167

point that I knew something had to be done concerning the growing mutant problem. By then, I was able to take control of an uninspired cog in the W. H. O. Under my guidance, the affairs of Mankind have progressed to this level." It spoke this last with an air of serene satisfaction.

Holly found her voice. "But why? Why send so many innocent people to die?"

"Not necessarily to die, my lady, but, in answer to your question, the percentage of mutant to natural human beings is alarmingly high at a time when the race needs to unite under a single leadership to stave off stagnation."

She wouldn't accept this. "But we could be changed, with electrolysis and plastic surgery."

With a flick of one reed-like hand, the machine in which it sat moved to face us a little more squarely. "Ah, but your genes, my dear, your genes. Are they changed by these corrective measures? No. Naturally, a good portion of the mutant population cannot conceive viable offspring. Two fine examples are in this room: though benignly hermaphroditic, I could never bear children, and, as much as you desire a baby of your own, you are irrevocably sterile, Miss Gylbre, according to your file.

"However, a surprising number of mutants *are* capable of normal reproduction with a moderately good chance of passing on the mutation. Mr. Harper, for instance, is such. Left unchecked, this would lead to an ever-growing sub-population of physically varient beings, a situation with all the potential to divide the Earth again."

"And you, good soul that you are, took it upon yourself to lead the blind masses from the wilderness?" I asked with rising sarcasm.

"Basically. Some one had to. Playing on the emotions of the normal section and spicing current events with occasional manufactured 'mutant uprisings,' I was able to achieve my primary goal."

"Why not extermination?"

"It didn't work for Hitler a hundred years ago, did it? Besides, there is no necessary reason for eliminating the entire faction for something they have no control over. On Thear, they can live out their lives in relative comfort as long as they don't progress to a plane making it possible to interfere with human expansion in the future."

"Or, simply, as long as they stay in their place, right?" All of my previous fear and awe was rapidly giving way to disgust.

"That may be oversimplification, but it is correct."

"Jeeze, how can a thing like you live in its own spoiled atmosphere this way?" I asked, forgetting my pains and standing tall. "What keeps the rot inside your skull from spilling out?"

The chair moved again, away this time. "You speak as if you were in control here," it said warily.

"I am, monster, and we both know that no electrified floor boards or hidden gun barrels can save you now." I took a step, feeling the charged portion of the floor with an instinctive mechanism and avoiding it. "You're very enthralling, almost persuasive, when you talk of uniting the human race and weeding out disruptive elements, but people have overcome differences many times before you and I appeared as accidents. Different tribes, different countries, different races, they all managed to work together and get us to the stars. And out there, we will find more people, and they won't pass 'God's Plan,' either. So we meet them as rational beings or we die."

"So naive," it said.

"I lost my naivete in a courtroom eighteen months ago, but I haven't lost my anger. You took more from me than that year and a half, more even than the lives of my friends. You took the girl I would have come to love and my father, and now you've got to pay. All of it."

The tiny hiss of a sliding panel alerted me to the danger of a stream of bullets from one wall, and I leaped safely aside, never stopping. My body had worked hard, stopping the bleeding from the gunshot and knitting almost all of my cuts. Though I wouldn't be well for a week or more, I was strong enough to do this one last duty.

"Try something else, you thing, something hard," I grinned.

Just like in the old serials, a gate of interlocking metal bars shot down from the ceiling to block my advance, but I gripped them in both hands, and, with two quick jerks, ripped out a portion large enough to walk through. Bullets spat at me again and missed just as badly. I was almost on it.

"You barbarous, idiotic fool!" the creature shouted. "You would meddle in the destiny of a complete race of beings using only sentimental drivel as a guide! Stop or I'll kill you where you stand!"

"Kill me," I said.

The wheelchair leaped back, heading for a rear exit that was just opening in the wall, but I caught hold of it before it got there and tipped the machine on its side. The creature spilled out like an aquatic thing on land. It writhed and tried to crawl from me on pitiful arms and legs.

"Stop, you lumbering cow!" it squealed. "You have no idea, no way of perceiving—"

With a scream, I grasped its doughy soft flesh and lifted it to face level. "You're dying! Die for all the damnation you've spread, the moral rot! Lord, die for Sheila and my father!"

Then it unleashed a mental bolt ten times more powerful than the one I'd felt on Thear. I collapsed like a sack of potatoes and began to jump in physical hysteria, as it tried to push *me* aside to invade my body. I lashed back with my own mind and, though powerful, my attack was too nebulous and unrefined to stop the sharply concentrated assault thrown against me. It was like trying to stop a one pound steel ball by throwing ten pounds of feathers at it.

"Submit!" the creature's brain screamed at me as it probed. "Must control... strong, very strong... must gain physical management... could never hope to fight in female's body... submit!"

For a moment, as I clawed my nails out on the floor, I thought it had given up; the weight was suddenly reduced from my mind, but it quickly renewed the assault with a grim new purpose. The object was no longer to control me, but to nip the very life from my body.

I was dying, and I knew it. Lying on my right side before the huddled monstrosity, I was having the energy drained from my soul and getting weaker every second, unable to move a weighty and sparkless form. Holly was there in my view, screaming silently, but I could only stretch out one hand to her in a wordless plea for help. She couldn't move due to the fear that filled her.

Get away, my brain commanded, get away, get away!

In that instant, the view of Holly's face locked in my eyes, eliminating all other sights, and the green skin, blue eyes, and white hair monopolized my thoughts.

Get away! Get away!

The face grew and filled my vision, the small nose becoming a shiny green boulder. My head pounded inside.

Get away! *Get away!*

Then... ahhhyyy!... nothingness, death... re-entry, and I was seeing again, looking at *my own face*. My body lay on the floor not fifteen feet away with wide, staring eyes, and the thing that had controlled Kurtz was there beside me, shouting, cursing, and trying to kill me.

But, here, this me watching it all had an aching neck and sore lips. It had long white hair falling beside its eyes. It had green...

"Oh my God!" I screamed in a cartoon character voice. I had transferred!

Not Holly, she couldn't help! Thumper!

I/Holly looked wildly for the ape man and saw him lying by the door where he had fallen after stepping on the electrified floor panel. Thumper had strength, Thumper had teeth, and ... Thumper was dead.

I was trapped in the form I had taken, and the thing was killing the real me, so I stumbled up. As Elias Harper, I had never felt heavy and seldom tired, because of muscles designed for weights far greater than my own, but in this form, I could barely stand upright and was almost overcome by a wave of dizziness. How could I save myself from this gross and inhuman beast? Not with the sure, powerful attack of Cat Harper, as my disbelieving consciousness was demanding. I had to have help.

The thing was laughing now, nearly finished with its task.

In desperation, I finally saw the overturned wheelchair and forced the emerald flesh to take me there. The cart ran on a self-contained power pack fixed to the underside of it and could be guided on "automatic pilot" by the special strips running along the floor. But when I tried to release the pack, I ran into trouble with the short, weak fingers. With the help of a strip of metal used as a pry bar on the wing nuts, I was able to unbolt the battery from its carriage and lug it—it weighed at least fifty pounds—across the room.

Like old-fashioned electric batteries, the energy of the pack was supplied by a chemical-solid reaction brought about by acids contained within, but these were extremely strong acids. Unscrewing the plastic caps on the top, I tilted the pack above the laughing creature and poured two gallons of acid directly into its face.

Screams of pure agony erupted in ear shattering blasts when the liquid burned into the thing below, and I dropped the casing of the pack into it to try to shut out the noise. The creature that was and wasn't William Kurtz flopped on the floor in death pains, while the acid ate deeper into it at each moment. A drop splashed on the leg I could now feel, and I cried out myself in a short, painful shout. But watching "Kurtz" die forced any other thoughts from me.

After a long time, at least five minutes, the shrieks faded into continuous groans and the frantic convulsions subsided into shivering. Then the groans and shivers passed, leaving only loud gulps for air, and, finally, silence. After too many deaths and too much sorrow, the Director of the World Health Organization expired, a burned, unrecognizible mass of formless flesh.

I nearly passed out as I stood in the quiet cell. My mind told me that I still carried a bullet in my midsection, which set more waves of fiery agony raging. When my hands touched smooth, cold skin, this realization was as terrible as the pain. I began mumbling in that ridiculous tone while I stooped to lift my motionless body from the floor, and again my confusion betrayed me, as the weight pulled me to my knees. These new muscles weren't equal to the job.

I was still kneeling there when Jeff and Ellen found the room and were stopped by the blue energy that guarded the door.

"Caribou!" Jeff shouted. "Let us in!"

I looked up dully.

"Turn the juice off!"

"Hi, Jeff," I said, "Thumper's dead. I think maybe I am, too. And Holly. I don't know what the hell's right anymore."

"She's in shock," explained Ellen. "Listen, honey, you've got to let us in so we can help you."

"Too late," I laughed. "Finnegan's dead, and the *thing* is dead. I killed them."

"You killed Finnegan?" was her incredulous question.

"Beat 'im to death."

"Shock," Ellen repeated.

I stumbled to an intricate control panel near the pack of the room, feeling strangely dizzy, and began to flip all of the "on" switches into the "off" position. In quick succession, I turned off the lights, raised the ceiling bars, stopped the air conditioning, and cleared the doorway.

"Are you all right?" Ellen asked as they rushed in.

"I hurt a lot," I admitted, walking to my body.

"Is Cat alive," said Jeff beside me.

I had one terrifying moment of rising, claustrophobic panic before I detected a faint heartbeat in the bloodstained chest. "Yeah, barely." At least I had a slim chance.

"What was that?"

I followed Ellen's trembling finger to the blackened mass that had been the mutant. "It was hell and the reason we were sentenced to Thear. But Kurtz is still alive up there with Doc guarding him, and he's going to change a lot of things if he wants to stay live."

"Jeeze, she's found a backbone," chuckled Jeff as he lifted my body. "Let's get old deadhead here up to a doctor before he decides to take the easy way out."

Ellen easily lifted me to my feet and helped me out the door behind Jeff, all the while trying to sooth my hurt. Pain ate at me all over, and blond hair continually fell into my eyes, but I was quietly happy. Mankind was free again, and the new James William Kurtz would rapidly change its course; the other mutant minds could be brought out of hiding to aid in the rebirth, while a galaxy of fresh worlds and races awaited us. Some questions nagged at me: if I could make the re-transference, could I bring Holly back from wherever she was now? Would the inhabitants of Thear accept and desire repatriation? Were there any more "things" waiting out there?

Still, I couldn't help but feel a kind of tired, sad triumph as we left the ruins below Rockefeller Center for another life in the sunshine above.

STARSPINNER
By Dale Aycock

PRICE: $2.25 LB973
CATEGORY: Science Fiction

AN EMPIRE FACES DEATH!

In the 27th century, travel over vast distances takes merely an instant—a terrifying, gut-gripping instant. Pilot Christopher Marlow must navigate spacecraft through a dangerous time/space warp called the "rim."

Substance X

"DAVID HOUSTON SHOWS A MATURITY AND WRITING TALENT WHICH COULD BE THE ENVY OF VETERANS OF A DOZEN NOVELS!"
—Amazing Magazine

SUBSTANCE X

LEISURE
$2.25

DAVID HOUSTON
Award-winning author of
ALIEN PERSPECTIVE
ILLUSTRATED

Working secretly in a Texas coastal village, a scientist uses the townsfolk as guinea pigs in an experiment designed to liberate mankind: he has invented a substance made of plankton and sea water that supplies all human nutritional needs. It also affects taste buds, nerves and memory.

By David Houston

PRICE: $2.25
0-8439-0961-7
CATEGORY: Science Fiction

SEND TO: **LEISURE BOOKS**
P.O. Box 511, Murry Hill Station
New York, N.Y. 10156-0511

Please send the titles:

Quantity	Book Number	Price
_____	_____	_____
_____	_____	_____
_____	_____	_____
_____	_____	_____
_____	_____	_____

In the event we are out of stock on any of your
selections, please list alternate titles below.

_____	_____	_____
_____	_____	_____
_____	_____	_____
_____	_____	_____

Postage/Handling_____

I enclose_____

FOR U.S. ORDERS, add 75¢ for the first book and 25¢ for
each additional book to cover cost of postage and handling.
Buy five or more copies and we will pay for shipping. Sorry,
no. C.O.D.'s.

FOR ORDERS SENT OUTSIDE THE U.S.A., add $1.00
for the first book and 50¢ for each additional book. PAY BY
foreign draft or money order drawn on a U.S. bank, payable
in U.S. ($) dollars.

☐ Please send me a free catalog.

NAME _____

(Please print)

ADDRESS _____

CITY _____ STATE _____ ZIP_____

Allow Four Weeks for Delivery